## Praise for the Regency Romances of Martha Kirkland

### A Perfect Scoundrel

"Engaging characters and a totally satisfying resolution. A Regency love story that will delight readers."
—Deborah Smith, author of
*The Stone Flower Garden*

### An Inconvenient Heir

"Kirkland perfectly paces this tightly woven, well-crafted story to keep readers turning pages to discover the next piece of the puzzle."      —*Romantic Times*

### Miss Wilson's Reputation

"A sparkling multifaceted gem of love and larceny. Martha Kirkland spins a free-spirited and fanciful tale of a feisty heroine, a fashionable hero, and a flamboyant villain."      —*Romantic Times*

### Miss Maitlin's Letters

"A talented author . . . a fine cast of characters . . . most enjoyable."      —*The Romance Reader*

### An Uncommon Courtship

"A clever piece of work from one of the top mistresses of the Regency genre."
—Inscriptions Magazine

### An Honorable Thief

"Ms. Kirkland exquisitely crafts a heartwarming romance, creating full-bodied characters for a fresh and original tale of love in olden times."
—*Romantic Times*

# A Perfect Scoundrel

## Martha Kirkland

A SIGNET BOOK

SIGNET
Published by New American Library, a division of
Penguin Group (USA) Inc., 375 Hudson Street,
New York, New York 10014, U.S.A.
Penguin Books Ltd, 80 Strand,
London WC2R 0RL, England
Penguin Books Australia Ltd, 250 Camberwell Road,
Camberwell, Victoria 3124, Australia
Penguin Books Canada Ltd, 10 Alcorn Avenue,
Toronto, Ontario, Canada M4V 3B2
Penguin Books (N.Z.) Ltd, Cnr Rosedale and Airborne Roads,
Albany, Auckland 1310, New Zealand

Penguin Books Ltd, Registered Offices:
80 Strand, London WC2R 0RL, England

First published by Signet, an imprint of New American Library,
a division of Penguin Group (USA) Inc.

First Printing, January 2004
10  9  8  7  6  5  4  3  2  1

PUBLISHER'S NOTE
This is a work of fiction. Names, characters, places, and incidents either are
the product of the author's imagination or are used fictitiously, and any resemblance to actual persons, living or dead, business establishments, events, or
locales is entirely coincidental.

*To some very special members
of the Georgia Romance Writers—
Denise Houser, Julie Dykstra,
Debby Giusti, and Emily Sewell*

# Chapter One

"*N*o, Tony. Not this time."

"But, Alex, I—"

"Save your breath. I said I would not do it, and I meant it."

Major Alexander Portman returned his brother's surprised stare. How easy it was for Tony to ask this favor of him. But then, life had always been easy for Tony. School, sports, friendships, beautiful women— nothing was ever beyond his reach. Their grandfather's heir by virtue of having come into the world twelve and a half minutes before his twin, Anthony William Portman could charm the birds from the trees in mere minutes. Charming women out of their clothes required even less time.

Unfortunately, Alex had much in common with those mindless birds, for he was not immune to his brother's charm. From their nursery days, Alex had found himself drawn into all Tony's foolish pranks and harebrained schemes, ever a willing participant. Now, for the first time in years, he looked into Tony's face— a face nearly identical to his own—and wondered if his brother would ever grow up.

Tony did not even notice the scrutiny; he merely tossed the playing cards he held onto the small mahogany games table and looked beseechingly at his brother. "I vow, Alex, I do not understand your reluctance. After all, it is not as though I am asking you to do something we have not done dozens of times."

"Dozens?" Alex could not decide whether to utter the profanity that sprang to his mind, or merely to laugh at his brother's selective memory. "My dear Tony, you were always one for underestimating the number of pranks for which you were directly responsible." He laid his own cards facedown on the table. "As for the canings we both received as a result of those pranks, I have lost count of the times I could not sit down to eat my dinner."

A spark of anger flashed in Tony's blue-gray eyes. "And when did you become the keeper of the tally? For that matter, when did you become such an old stick? All I am asking is a day or two out of your life. A week at the most."

This latest favor was far too reminiscent of the pranks the brothers had pulled when still schoolboys, so why had Alexander been so surprised by the request? Perhaps because this was not some Latin exam for which Tony had not studied. They were at school no longer, and with their thirtieth birthday only months away, a sensible person might expect a bit more maturity from the pair who had been scamps from the first day they drew breath.

Though they were identical twins, the order of their births had dictated the course of their lives. As the firstborn son, Anthony was the heir. His life was preordained, for one day he would step into their grandfather's shoes. Tony would be the sixth Baron Bevin, entrusted with all the wealth and power that accompanied that title. As for Alexander, the second-born son, he had been expected to choose a profession, which he had. After eight years in His Majesty's service, however, he had had enough of war. Just three weeks ago he had resigned his commission in an oft-decorated Guards regiment.

The brothers had not seen each other for more than two years. Because of all Alex had experienced—the senseless destruction of humans and property, the comrades lost—the years had wrought an enormous change in him. Those same years seemed to have had little effect upon the heir.

"Why not do me this one little favor?" Tony asked. "Be a sport. You said you meant to go down to Portman Park as soon as your business in town was completed. What difference can it make if you go a bit earlier than planned?"

"The difference is that I meant to visit our grandfather as myself, not while pretending to be my twin brother. I have questions to ask Grandfather about the running of an estate."

"Estates. Bah. Leave the details to your steward. Boring business that."

"To you, perhaps. You have always known you would inherit Portman Park, and as a consequence you have been instructed in the day-to-day operation of such a property. My recent inheritance was totally unexpected, and I am far too appreciative of the house and lands our mother's uncle left me to wish to see them lose value because of my lack of experience. I realize I have much to learn, but if I can be half the landlord our grandfather is, my tenants will have no reason to complain."

"A worthy sentiment," Tony said, employing a tone whose sincerity had been honed to perfection in his youth, "and one that does you justice." He smiled sweetly at his brother, the smile causing a dimple to appear in his left cheek.

"Oh, no! Not the dimple!" Alexander made a cross

of his hands in front of his face, as if to protect himself from some Gypsy's curse. "Anything but the dimple."

Unable to stop themselves, both brothers laughed.

"I beg of you, Tony, save your smiles for use on someone who has not seen every weapon in your arsenal. I know you too well, and nothing you can say or do will induce me to pretend to be you."

Tony pushed his chair back, rose from the games table, and walked over to the slate fireplace. August was not yet over, but the evenings were growing noticeably chilly, and the small fire Ottway had lit was welcome. The bachelor's rooms, located above a tobacconist's shop on a side street just off Piccadilly, were on loan to his brother from one of his comrades in arms, but as usual, Ottway, Alexander's batman, had done his best to make the three small rooms comfortable. "You cannot take Ottway with you," Tony said, "for Grandfather would recognize that granite-faced Welshman in a trice."

"How fortunate, then, that I have no intention of going—"

"As luck would have it," Tony said, completely ignoring his brother's continued refusals, "I have a new valet, one the old gentleman has not clamped eyes on yet, so it would be no problem to—"

"Another valet? How many is that? Eight? Ten? Caesar's ghost, Tony, have you still not learned how to deal with your—"

"No lectures! Not from you. You do not know what my life is like. With Grandfather forever preaching at me to marry and begin filling the nursery with a score of squalling brats, and every matchmaking mama in town throwing her horse-faced daughter at my feet, I haven't a moment's peace."

"Peace? Is that what you want? Forgive me if I have misjudged you, but somehow I had it in mind that you wanted to take in a mill with a few of your care-for-nought friends. Accompanied, of course, by a certain barque of frailty with improbable red hair and an equally unlikely name."

Tony chuckled. "So, you have seen the lovely Cerise."

"I have."

Tony kissed his fingertips. "Is she not a goddess?"

"Having had little association with divinities, I cannot answer that. In truth, she does possess a most impressive bosom—one, I daresay, that would turn any man's head—but aside from that feature, I detected nothing so special about her that your conquest could not be postponed for a week or so."

"Nothing special! Good God, brother, you have become an old stick!"

"Perhaps. But I see no reason why you cannot do as our grandfather asks. Mr. Quick is an old friend, and if, as you say, he and Mrs. Quick intend to remain at Portman Park for only a matter of days, meeting his family should not be such an onerous task."

"He has two unmarried daughters," Tony said, as if that explained everything. Which, of course, it did.

Alexander knew the *ton* considered his brother a *premier parti*. Tony was heir to a distinguished title and would one day be a very wealthy man, but aside from that he was both charming and handsome. Though there was only one person in the world who could tell one twin from the other, Tony was far the handsomer. It was something that came from inside him, some mysterious quality that had been his at birth.

Both brothers were six feet tall, with dark brown hair and blue-gray eyes, but Tony's features were slightly more classical, his profile softer and more appealing to the ladies. Alexander's jawline was sharper, the shape of his nose far from perfect, and his eyebrows were straight, practically meeting over his eyes, while Tony's brows were handsomely curved.

Furthermore, Tony possessed the lean, graceful physique of the gentleman-sportsman, while Alexander's body was far more muscular, mainly because he had led a soldier's rigorous life. And like most soldiers, he had a tanned complexion, while his brother's penchant for life among the *ton,* with its daily excesses of wine, women, and late nights, lent him an interesting pallor, the sort females found romantic.

Interesting? Romantic? Alexander felt a bit queasy at the thought. Perhaps he *had* become an old stick, but the last thing in the world he wanted was the *ton* life. Gambling, drinking oneself into oblivion, simpering females on the catch for a rich husband, none of these things held the least appeal for him.

Misreading his brother's silence, Tony said, "I understand that both Mr. Quick's daughters are blonde. You always liked blondes. And from what I hear, one of the girls is rather pretty. Certainly pretty enough to interest a fellow who has been in the Peninsula, fighting Boney's soldiers for the past two years and presumably deprived of female companionship."

Alex shook his head. "The answer is still no. I have said I will not be a party to this childish prank, and nothing you can say or do will change my mind." Noting that flash of anger again, Alex warned his brother to keep his displeasure in check. "Have a care, Tony, for I am in no mood to put up with one of your fits of temper."

"Oh? And what would you do? Toss me out on my ear?"

"If need be," he replied quietly.

Ever a hothead, Tony began unbuttoning his waistcoat, his movements deliberate, his purpose unmistakable. "You think you can best me?"

Alex stood, not the least intimidated by the challenge. "I can," he said softly, "and you and I both know it."

It was as well for the peace of the house that Ottway heard a disturbance outside on the stairs and came at a run to fling open the door. "Sir!" he said, calling to his master, "it's Captain Lansdale. He's been hurt. All over blood, he be."

Alex rushed to the corridor, arriving just in time to catch his friend as he collapsed. "Lansdale! I have you," he said. "You are safe now."

"Alex? Is that you?"

"It is, old fellow."

"No place else to turn," the captain said, clutching at Alex's lapels. "Knew you would help me. Sorry for the inconvenience, but—"

"Put a sock in it, Lansdale. Where else should you turn, if not to me? And though I am curious to know how a fellow who survived legions of French soldiers let himself be felled by a bit of homegrown mayhem, pray, do not give me the story straightaway. Instead, let me get you inside where I can assess the damage."

After lifting his slender comrade in his arms, he carried him into the parlor and laid him on the settee, placing a pillow beneath the blond hair that was liberally streaked with blood. A cut just above the captain's right eye bled profusely, sending red rivulets down his face. Judging by the egg-sized knot at the back of his head, and the bruises that were already beginning to show color, not to mention the way he was hugging himself to protect his ribs, he had obviously been set upon by more than one man.

"Damnation," the injured man said suddenly, staring at the tall gentleman who leaned against the mantel, watching the proceedings with only mild interest. "I must be worse off than I thought, Alex, for I see two of you."

"My brother," Alex said, waving a negligent hand toward his sibling.

The ever-efficient Ottway, wasting no time with foolish questions, had rushed to the small kitchen only to return within a matter of minutes bearing a tray containing a roll of bandages, several thick towels, and a shaving bowl filled with water. "With your permission, Captain Lansdale, I'll see what I can do to stop the bleeding."

The captain's wounds, though serious, were not of a life-threatening nature, and after suffering Ottway's ministrations, then downing a full snifter of brandy, Lansdale was able to relate an abridged version of what had happened to him. "Since selling out," he began, "I haven't known what to do with myself. I'm not one of those downy fellows who likes to read and take in the museums, so I . . . I've been playing the fool in a manner best suited to the rawest of green recruits."

This particular bit of information came as no surprise to Alex. Geofrey Lansdale was as brave a soldier as ever lived, for he feared nothing and no one, and he was always ready to lead the charge. Unfortunately, that same rash quality that served him on the battlefield betrayed him when it came to living in the real world. He acted first and thought later, not a wise course of action—especially where one's civilian enemies were not so obliging as to wear a uniform so they were distinguishable from one's friends.

"To make a long story short," the captain continued, "I fell in with a set of Greek *banditti,* and now I owe a great deal of money to one of them—a rather nasty character called Frank Worldly. Though considering his accent, I doubt that is his real name."

"Certainly not the one his mother gave him," Tony said. "Though you have to admit it's an apt name for a card sharp."

Alex gave his brother a quelling look, then bid Lansdale continue with his story.

"I was to have settled my debt yesterday, but I, er, missed the appointment."

"You missed it?" Alex asked, skepticism in his voice. "Not very wise of you, old fellow."

"Most unwise," Tony added. "But from the look of you, I would guess that some of Worldly's men showed you the error of your ways."

The captain nodded, then winced at the pain this movement caused. "After impressing upon me the importance of not being late a second time, they informed me that Worldly has given me until day after tomorrow to bring him the money, plus ten percent interest."

"How much do you owe?" Alex asked. "I am assuming you cannot put your hands on sufficient money. Perhaps I could lend—"

"No. You cannot, for the man holds my vowels for ten thousand pounds."

At the same time, Alex and Tony whistled.

"I know, I know," Lansdale said, burying his throbbing face in his hands. "In retrospect, I believe the play was crooked."

Tony muttered something beneath his breath about those lacking sufficient town bronze being turned loose without a keeper. "Pigeons ripe for the plucking," he said.

Alex chose to remain silent. There was no changing the circumstances, and Lansdale had, indeed, been a pigeon ripe for the plucking. As it happened, however, Alex owed his life to this particular pigeon, for Geoffrey Lansdale had pulled him from beneath a dead horse when others had already passed him by, leaving him on the battlefield to die. For that reason, if there was anything he could do for his friend, Alex felt honor-bound to do it.

To explain his foolish behavior, the captain continued with his story. "At first I won almost every hand. It was as though Lady Luck was sitting in the chair beside me, her guiding hand on my shoulder. Night after night I was victorious. Small amounts at first, then before I knew it I had amassed more than a thousand pounds."

He looked up at last, the swollen lower lip and the bandage-swathed head lending added pathos to his embarrassment. "I should have stopped while I was ahead, but it was unbelievably exciting, sitting there each night, with dozens of men crowded around the table, cheering me on as I outwitted far more seasoned players. Whist. Vingt-et-un. No matter what game I chose to play, I was the big winner."

He laughed, then gasped as the action tugged at his tender lip. "I don't suppose I need tell you that my luck suddenly changed?"

"No," Alex replied quietly, "you need not."

"Actually, it is an all-too-familiar story," Tony informed the injured man. "The yahoos who run the gaming hells know just how long to play a fish before they reel him in. Unfortunately, a gaming debt, no matter where it is run up, is still a debt of honor, and a gentleman must pay."

"Gentleman be damned!" the captain said. "I cannot pay. Not now, at any rate. If I had more time, I could get in touch with my father. He would ring a royal peal over me, of course, but he would pay. No matter how angry Father becomes, he knows how it would affect my lady mother to have her youngest son found floating facedown in the Thames."

He turned back to Alex. "As luck would have it, my father is on a walking trip in Wales until the end of the month, so I cannot get word to him of my troubles. That is why I came to you. I need a place to hide until my father returns."

Alex was quick to give his assurance of a place to stay. "You may remain here as long as you like."

"No. These rooms will not do. For all I know, the men who beat me may have followed me here. The day after tomorrow, when I do not take Worldly his ten thousand, chances are good that this will be the first place those nasty devils look for me."

He said nothing more, yet his hopeful expression

silently implored his friend to suggest something that would meet his needs.

Tony was the first to offer a suggestion. "The captain will require a place where Frank Worldly's men would never think to look for him. Of course, it must be a truly secluded spot. Preferably, one as far from town as possible."

Alex stared at his brother, mistrusting his sudden interest in another's plight.

"Do you know of such a place?" Captain Lansdale asked. "Some hunting lodge or a cottage in the country? Even an abandoned crofter's hut would do, for I am not the least bit nice in my notions. Ask Alex. He will tell you that he and I have billeted in far worse places."

Tony stepped forward, a smile on his lips. "As it happens, my dear Captain, I am persuaded I know just the place. One where no one would think to look for you. It may need a thorough cleaning, of course, but the place I have in mind would be far more comfortable than some abandoned hut."

A quiver of relief ran through Geofrey Lansdale's bruised body. "Thank Heaven. Sir, you have saved my life. Pray, where is this refuge, and how soon may I go there? The sooner the better, for I don't mind telling you I would as leave not meet those yahoos again until I have the money in hand."

"The place to which I refer is located in Hampshire, on the edge of the New Forest, in a little riverside village called Buckler's Hard. And the refuge I offer you is the dower house—a cottage, actually—at Portman Park, on my estate."

"*Your* estate?" Alex said. "At last report, the property, including Auntie's Cottage, still belonged to Grandfather."

Tony gave a negligent wave of his hand. "Semantics, brother dear. Mere semantics."

Alex was not fooled for an instant by his brother's

casual manner. "You think yourself a very clever fellow, Tony, but I am fully cognizant of what you hope to accomplish with this proposal. And I tell you, it will not work." His voice was cold, but the anger in his eyes flashed hotly, warning his brother not to push him too far.

Tony ignored the warning; instead, he returned his attention to Geofrey Lansdale. "As for how soon you may leave this coldhearted and exceedingly dangerous city, Captain, that decision rests entirely with my brother. As luck would have it, just before you arrived Alexander and I were discussing the possibility of his traveling down to Portman Park to pay his respects to our grandfather."

"Truly?" A sigh of relief was dragged from the wounded man, the shaky sound not unlike that of a man snatched from the very jaws of hell. "Heaven be praised, for I thought all was lost."

When Alex made no reply, merely glowered at his brother, Tony's smile broadened in triumph and out popped that dimple. "What say you, Alex? Ready to travel to Hampshire?"

"Damn you, Tony!"

Tony laughed aloud. "I knew you would not let me down."

"I am not doing it for you."

His twin shrugged his elegantly clad shoulders. "Your reasons do not concern me. I care only that you agree to the plan."

"Of that, I have no doubt. Nothing matters to you except that you get your own way. But have a care, Tony, for one day one of your pranks will go awry, and when that day comes, I hope you will still be able to smile."

Not in the least penitent, Tony threw his arms around his brother's neck and all but throttled him. "You are truly the best of brothers," he said, for all the world as if they had come to an amicable arrangement. "And you have my promise that I shall come to relieve you of the impersonation in just a few days."

"You had better."

"My word on it. A few days. A week at the most."

# Chapter Two

*August 21*
*Buckler's Hard, Hampshire*

*J*uliet Moseby fled across the timeworn marble floor of the Portman Park vestibule, anger prompting her to yank open the heavy oak door before one of the footmen could rush to her aid. Not caring that the servant witnessed her unladylike behavior, she muttered an oath better suited to a stable lad, then slammed the door behind her.

Once past the recessed entry of the sprawling Elizabethan house, she did not pause, merely continued down the single step, then ran down the pleached walk, under its dome-like, interlaced beech branches. The day had been overcast, and now a light drizzle fell, and though the branches of the trees protected her from the moisture, nothing protected her slipper-clad feet from the bite of the crushed stone.

Such was her anger that she felt nothing. She saw nothing. Not the beauty of the park grounds, with their six hundred–plus acres of unspoiled woodland, not the nature trails, not the bridle paths, nor even the celebrated knot garden that was reputed to be the work of the famed Capability Brown. Her fury blinded her to all but the avenue overhung by two-hundred-year-old beech trees.

"How dare she," she muttered, giving vent to her emotions, though usually she remained impassive, protected by a cocoon of her own making. "That . . . that viper!"

It was not as though Juliet had never heard herself referred to as someone's natural daughter; after all, her lineage was no secret, surely all of Hampshire knew of her birth. Furthermore, she had had twenty-six years in which to become inured to the derogatory terms, as well as to the smirks that often accompanied the remarks. It was just that she had not expected to hear herself called a bastard at Portman Park, a place where she had thought herself among friends.

The old adage about eavesdroppers had proven true, for she had heard nothing good of herself. Not that she had meant to listen to the guests' conversation. Unfortunately, she suspected that Mrs. Quick had meant for her to overhear.

By design, Juliet had completed her toilette well before time for family and guests to gather for sherry in the music room, a cozy retreat that had been a favorite of the baron's late wife, and she had gone down early in hopes of finding Tony there, alone. As a friend of long standing, she felt she owed it to him to warn him about the plans afoot to ensnare him in parson's mousetrap. As it happened, she was not the only person with a wish to be the first to speak to the heir, for Hermione Quick and her two daughters were there before her.

Juliet had just entered the small anteroom to the left of the vestibule, and because that chamber gave access to the music room, where the door stood ajar, she had heard every word being spoken. "I vow," Mrs. Quick said, "I have never been so insulted in my life." The faded beauty's plump, matronly bosom quivered with outrage. "To be expected to sit down to dinner with that . . . that *creature* is the outside of enough."

"But, Mama," her youngest daughter said, knowing

immediately to whom her mother referred, "she is Lady Featherstone's ward—or she was for the years of her adolescence—and with her ladyship acting as Lord Bevin's hostess, one can hardly expect Miss Moseby to be excluded from the—"

"I can and I do expect it," Miss Celeste's mama informed her. "The creature is someone's by-blow, call her what you will, and I did not come to Hampshire to be subjected to such base-born company. It is unconscionable, and if your father had the least strength of character, he would insist that Lord Bevin send her packing."

Miss Celeste made a *shush*ing sound. "Mama, I pray you, hold your tongue. You know how excitable Papa is, and you might well provoke an argument irrevocably injurious to us all."

"To us? Have you taken leave of your senses?"

"No, ma'am, I have not. Only think what you are saying, then remember why we have come here. Father's debts."

"Do not speak to me of your father's debts, for I am all too aware of them. Have they not hung over my head these twenty years and more like the sword of that Greek fellow?"

"Damocles," Miss Beatrice Quick said. "Though, in truth, Mama, the sword that threatened Damocles hung over his head by a single hair, threatening immediate decapitation."

"Gentlemen," the young lady's mother informed her in a voice stiff with censure, "do not admire girls who exhibit book learning."

"Father's debts," Miss Celeste continued, in an attempt to bring the conversation back to the subject, "have reached the point where something must be done about them. Unfortunately, the only idea anyone has come up with for paying them off—the only suggestion that seems at all likely of accomplishing that

Herculean task—is for my sister and me to marry well."

"Hercules," Miss Beatrice offered for her mother's edification, "was a Greek hero who—"

"Will you be still," her mama said. "I do not see what any of those Greeks has to do with my quite understandable annoyance at having this Moseby creature flung in our faces. I still say if your father—"

"Concentrate, Mama. What if Papa should anger the old gentleman and it is us, and not Miss Moseby, who is asked to quit the Park? Beatrice and I might never come to the attention of Anthony Portman, who, as you know, is the most marriageable *parti* in England. If we miss this opportunity, and Papa should put his spoon in the wall—"

Mrs. Quick gasped. "Spoon in the wall! Celeste, I forbid you to use such a vulgar expression."

"Your pardon, Mama, but no matter what expression I use, the truth remains. If Papa should die— heaven forbid!—while still owing every tradesman in the kingdom, we may well be ruined. Of a certainty we will be turned out of our home, perhaps with only what we can carry in our hands. Without suitable dowries, my sister and I will likely remain spinsters, while you will be left with only your modest jointure to see you through your remaining years."

When applied to Mrs. Quick, the name was a misnomer. Even so, the woman was not such a slow top that she did not turn ashen-faced at the thought of being thrown from her home, obliged to survive on nothing more than a widow's portion.

"Our mother cares nothing for the future," Miss Beatrice Quick said, a hint of sarcasm in her voice. "She values her pride above all else. And why should she not? After all, what are Papa's plans to introduce us to Lord Bevin's heir when compared with the ignominy of sitting at table with a young woman who enjoys the obvious affection of our hostess, the dowager Lady Featherstone, and the friendship of our host?"

Hermione Quick appeared delighted to abandon thoughts of near poverty and turn her attention to the shortcomings of her oldest daughter. "I will thank you, miss, to remain silent! *The friendship of our host* indeed! Much you know of the matter, or of gentlemen and their ways. You, who have squandered two seasons in town. Two very expensive seasons, I might add, without bringing even one eligible gentleman to the sticking point!"

Like most fair-skinned blondes, Miss Beatrice could not hide her embarrassment, for her pretty face turned a deep pink. "My deficiencies notwithstanding, Mama, I know enough to assure you that Tony Portman would not look kindly upon the daughters of a man who had insulted the old gentleman in his own home."

This observation being unanswerable, Mrs. Quick returned to the subject of their hostess's ward. "I still say we should not be subjected to that Moseby person's company. Her mother was clearly no better than she should be, and it is a proven fact that the apple does not fall far from the tree. Why, it would not surprise me to discover that Juliet Moseby is Tony Portman's mistress, and that he and that . . . that *bastard* are carrying on a liaison beneath this very roof."

"Mama!" Miss Celeste said, "I beg of you, say no more. Anyone might hear you."

Juliet did not wait to hear the vicious harridan's reply. Instead, she bit her lower lip to still the words she longed to utter, then turned and ran from the house, her anger all but choking her. *Tony's mistress!* How dare anyone say such a thing!

Over the years Juliet had been obliged to swallow more than one angry retort. She had learned early to conceal her hurt from prying eyes, to pretend that the snubs and whispered slurs did not find their way to her heart like so many barbed arrows.

For her own peace of mind, she had adopted a momentary deafness when entering a room where others had already begun conversations. Even so, Mrs. Quick's insult could not be ignored. Juliet might have been born on the wrong side of the blanket, but that was no fault of hers. A baby had no say in where he or she was born, and not by the least word or act of hers had Juliet Moseby ever given anyone reason to question her morals.

As for her mother, a dearer, kinder person never lived than Dora Tyler Moseby. And if there was, indeed, a heavenly reward, then her mother was there at this very moment, her gentle smile warming the hearts of Saint Peter and all the inhabitants of eternity.

Unfortunately, Juliet was not one of those heavenly residents. She resided here on Earth, where spiteful she-cats uttered thoughtless, cruel words without a care for the feelings of others.

Juliet wished she might run the mile and a half to Stone House and never return to Portman Park, certainly not while the Quicks remained; however, that haven was no longer hers. Stone House was no longer the refuge it had been for the past fourteen years of her life. Scarce a month after dear Sir Titus' death last Michaelmas, his heir, a distant cousin, had claimed his rights and taken up residence.

Since that time, the new baronet and his lady had done everything in their power to hasten Lady Featherstone's departure, making her feel an unwelcome guest in the home that had been hers for forty years. As for Juliet, they pretended she was invisible, speaking to her only when conversation could not be avoided.

Soon, however, thanks to Lord Bevin's generosity, she and dear Lady Feather would take up temporary residence in the Portman Park dower house—a structure referred to affectionately as *Auntie's Cottage*.

They would reside at the cottage only until spring, for as soon as the weather made travel advisable, they meant to remove to London.

As for the length of their stay in Town, that depended greatly upon the completion of the task Juliet had set herself. Actually, it was a quest, and because it was one she undertook for the sake of her mother's memory, Juliet meant to see that every last detail was carried out respectfully, deliberately, and without undue haste.

If it could be done, she meant to meet her father, face to face.

Once that initial feat was accomplished, it was her plan to look that supposed gentleman in the eye and demand to know why he had left her mother to bear her disgrace alone. If there were extenuating circumstances—and in the deepest reaches of her heart Juliet hoped there were—she wanted to hear them. The success or failure of that long-overdue meeting would determine how soon she and Lady Feather removed to one of the spa towns where they meant to set up permanent residence for themselves.

The months until spring would give the Bow Street officer Juliet had hired time to locate her father. In the meantime, she and Lady Feather would reside in Auntie's Cottage. His lordship's kind offer of the house, coupled with a friendship that spanned more than four decades, was the major reason Lady Feather had agreed to act as Lord Bevin's hostess for the duration of the Quicks' visit—a visit their host had done his best to discourage. Though he wished his heir to marry, his lordship expected Tony to know what was due his family name. Theirs was an old and well-respected name, and for that reason, his lordship was looking quite a bit higher than the Quicks for his future granddaughter-in-law.

Aware of his lordship's requirements, Juliet smiled.

Hermione Quick's schemes notwithstanding, neither of her daughters had much hope of becoming the next Lady Bevin. With only their pretty faces to recommend them, those two young ladies were scarcely more likely to join the illustrious Portman family than some gentleman's natural daughter.

Not that Juliet had ever entertained such a thought! She and the twins were friends. Nothing more.

Without realizing how far she had traveled, Juliet had arrived at the wide carriage drive that veered to left of the pleached walk. Ahead of her stood the cottage, which was slightly more than half a mile from the manor house. Situated just inside the walled entrance with its stuccoed arch, the cottage was nestled among a thicket of tall blackthorn hedges that had been allowed to grow with little or no interference from the Park's gardener.

In early spring, when the sloes were ripe, the cook sent servants to gather the fruit to make jellies and to flavor a sort of homemade gin employed in the colder weather to ward off the ague. Now, however, the thick green hedges served only to give character to an otherwise characterless edifice. Juliet slowed her pace, then paused to study the unpretentious structure that was to be her home for the next few months. Topped by a thatched roof, the red brick rectangle was not handsome, even when bathed in the twilight that had begun to streak the western sky with brushstrokes of pink, orange, and gold.

Unlike the main house, which was a three-hundred-year-old Elizabethan manor fashioned of flint bonded with white chalk, covered by a layer of stucco added by a subsequent baron, Auntie's Cottage, consisting of two floors and an attic, was a relatively new structure. Built by the present baron's father, the eight-room cottage had been occupied only for a short time by one of the baron's more eccentric maiden aunts.

That lady's tenancy had ended sixty years ago, and
since that time the cottage had remained empty.

Juliet had not the least idea when the building had
been inspected last for such things as roof leaks and
dry rot, but she had been assured by Lord Bevin's
housekeeper that it had been aired and given a thorough cleaning during the past week. Eager to see for
herself just what sort of condition the rooms were in,
she approached the narrow front door, with its simple
pediment, and lifted the latch.

The door hinges protested at being put into service
after so many years, but the squeaking noise did not
bother Juliet overmuch. What did bother her were the
muffled sounds that came from the upper floor, where
the four bedchambers were located. In addition to
hurried footfalls, she heard whispers. The voice was
unmistakably male; even so, Juliet was more annoyed
than frightened.

Her maid, Morag Browne, a Scotswoman who knew
every piece of neighborhood gossip worth knowing,
had warned Juliet that the cottage was a favorite
trysting place for the dairy maids and their swains.
Clearly, the trysters would be obliged to find a new
place for their assignations, and this moment was as
good a time as any to let them know that the new
tenants meant to take up residence within the next
sennight.

With that objective in mind, Juliet stood at the foot
of the narrow staircase, her hand resting on a carved
pineapple finial, and spoke into the contrived silence.
"Who is there?"

When there was no reply, she called again, slightly
louder. "Whoever you are, I have no wish to cause
trouble for anyone, so if you leave immediately there
will be no questions asked."

Still no reply. Not a sound.

"I heard you moving about and talking," she

shouted up the stairs, "so do not even try to pretend it was my imagination. You have exactly one minute to vacate the premises. Otherwise, I shall have no recourse but to fetch some of Lord Bevin's men to remove you bodily."

When there was still no reply, the anger that had begun with Mrs. Quick's cruel words resurfaced. Though Juliet knew her vexation was misplaced, she gripped the handrail with her right hand, used her left to lift the hem of her skirt so she did not trip, then hurried up the narrow, uncarpeted stairs, ready to give the intruders a piece of her mind.

A short corridor separated the upper rooms. Two bedchambers faced the carriageway and two faced the rear garden, but with the sun dropping behind the western horizon, the light was fading fast, leaving Juliet with scant clues as to what sort of furnishings lay within those rooms. Not that she needed light. Her nose told her that a candle flame had been extinguished only moments before, so she followed that unmistakable aroma down the darkening corridor to the door that gave access to the attic stairs.

The door was slightly ajar, but undesirous of confronting a couple who might not have had sufficient time to don any articles of clothing previously removed, she rapped sofly on the doorjamb. "Come out immediately," she said, "I will brook no more delay."

She heard nothing, though she sensed that someone was in the attic. Too late those same senses told her that another someone was behind her. By that time, however, a large hand had been clamped over her mouth, and an iron-hard arm had snaked around her midsection, pinning her arms to her sides. Before she had time to think, she was pulled rather roughly against a body that was rock solid and imposing enough to make her knees threaten to give way beneath her.

"*You* will brook no more delay? And what gives you the right to be issuing orders?" he asked, his whispered words and warm breath tickling her ear. "Is this your trysting place? Are you one of the Park dairy maids come to meet your lover?"

Juliet's arms were hopelessly pinned, and when she attempted to kick her captor's shins, in hopes of making him release her, she succeeded in hurting only herself. Damp slippers were no match for sturdy leather top boots, and she soon realized she could do nothing to make this tall, powerful man let her go. Nor could she prevent his next action. With his hand still clamped over her mouth, he slipped his pinning arm down to her hips for just a moment before moving it upward again until it was stopped by the weight of her bosom.

"Umm," he said, an unmistakable smile in his voice, "even soaked to the skin, you are a delectable armful, my dear, and if your face matches your curves, then your swain is to be congratulated. Unfortunately, I fear he will not be warming you this night. You and he must abandon this place for a time at least, for I have need of it for a few days."

Juliet was already wishing she had remained belowstairs, but now she wished it even more, for she recognized the speaker's voice. It was Tony Portman who held her captive. Tony taking liberties with her person!

He had said he had need of this place, and unless she missed her guess, he was up to another of his juvenile pranks when he should have been up at the manor house getting himself affianced. As far as Juliet was concerned, it would serve him right to become leg-shackled to one of the Misses Quick, so he might have that harridan for his mama-in-law.

For the moment, though, he still held Juliet prisoner against his body, and without easing his hold he turned and walked her down the corridor to the top of the stairs. "Now, sweeting," he said, "this is what I want you to do. I mean to let you go, but I want your word that you will not make a sound. If you promise to leave immediately and not tell a soul what has occurred here, I will give you a reward."

*Reward indeed!* As if she wanted anything from him.

Apparently he waited for some show of agreement from her. "Have I your promise?" he said.

Juliet could not decide which emotion was uppermost in her mind, her embarrassment at being manhandled, or her fury that it was Tony who had her within his control. In any event, she nodded to let him know that she would not scream.

As if satisfied with her nod, he freed her mouth, though he kept his arm around her, imprisoning her still.

While she attempted to catch her breath and bring her emotions under control, he reached inside his waistcoat pocket, extracted a coin, then without so much as a by-your-leave reached over her shoulder and dropped the coin down the low-cut front of her dinner dress. At the unexpected coldness of the metal she gasped. "Tony Portman, you lecher, unhand me this instant!"

For just a moment he remained perfectly still, then he added insult to injury by laughing out loud. "Is that you, Juliet?"

"You know it is I, you despicable excuse for a gentleman."

He laughed again, the sound vibrating deep within his chest. "Never tell me that Miss Serious is here to meet a secret lover. Not one of the footmen, I trust."

Oh! As if she would do anything so reprehensible! And how like Tony to remind her of the name the twins used to call her when she was a girl, a reminder that did nothing to improve her disposition. "Though it is none of your business, you unprincipled lout, I have no secret lover. Now unhand me."

"First," he said, amusement lacing his voice, "I wonder if I dare retrieve my coin. Surely you have no wish to keep—"

His amusement ended abruptly and, Juliet hoped painfully, for she had worked her arm free, and retaliating as she had done when still a child, she scraped her fingernails down the back of his hand.

"Damnation!" he muttered, letting her go at last, "you had no need to do that. You know I would never force myself upon a female."

"I know," she replied, her voice filled with disdain, "you were in jest. I have heard it all before, and I have no patience for your continued pranks." She turned now and looked up at him, though she could see little more than the outline of his features in the darkness. "I wonder, Tony, do you never mean to act in a manner befitting your age and station?"

Assuming that Juliet's question regarding Tony's maturity was rhetorical, Alex did not reply. For one thing, the insult was not meant for him, and for another, he was far too happy to find that she had accepted him as his brother to think of anything else. From their first meeting all those years ago, Juliet had been able to tell the twins one from the other. How she did it when no one else seemed capable of distinguishing Tony from Alex, he did not know. Now it appeared she had lost that knack, and for this he was grateful; he had enough to worry about these next few days.

"How is your hand?" she asked, bringing his thoughts back to the moment.

"I will live."

"I am relieved to hear it."

Since this was probably as much of an apology as he was likely to receive, he said nothing more, merely removed a linen handkerchief from inside his coat and pressed the folded square against the scratches, quite certain his captive had drawn blood. Not that he blamed her for defending herself, nor for being cross as crabs at what she perceived as a childish prank.

He had not meant to frighten her, of course, but he had been in dead earnest when he imprisoned her. Like her, he knew of the rumors that the servants used the cottage for their trysts, and he did not want one of the dairy maids or some overly randy footman stumbling across Geofrey Lansdale, who even now lay on one of the servant's cots in the attic, with Tony's new valet in attendance.

Geofrey's presence at Portman Park must remain a secret. Otherwise, Alex might not be able to keep him safe from the gallows birds who would soon be searching London for him. As for the mysterious Mr. Worldly, who had a reputation for ruthlessness, Alex dare not chance his finding Geofrey and making an example of him. There was no knowing to what lengths such a man might go to punish someone who failed to pay a ten-thousand-pound gaming debt.

To get Juliet away from the vicinity of the attic as quickly as possible, Alex put his arm beneath her elbow and began walking with her down the stairs. "I truly thought you were one of the dairy maids," he said by way of explanation for his actions, "and I apologize if I frightened you."

"I was not frightened."

"Of course not," he replied, his tone giving the lie to his words. "In these modern days, gently reared females are often grabbed from behind by unknown men. Why should you have been disturbed by so commonplace an event?"

"Spare me your sarcasm," she said, pulling her elbow free of his firm but polite grasp. "Instead, enlighten me if you will on a matter I find rather puzzling. Since your grandfather has been expecting you anytime this entire day, why are you here, skulking about the cottage?"

"I might ask the same of you."

"Ah, but it is *not* the same," she said. "For *I* was not skulking. I made my presence known as soon as I heard noise abovestairs. Besides, I have every right to be here."

"How so? This cottage is part of the Portman estate, and the last I heard anything of the matter, you resided at Stone House."

"If you must know, Lord Bevin has graciously invited Lady Feather and me to make our home here for as long as we wish."

"Now that is news," he said. "And though I am loath to pry into my neighbors' affairs, I do wonder what has occurred to make such a move desirable."

Receiving only a shrug of her shoulders for answer, Alex continued. "Since Lady Featherstone has a life interest in her late husband's estate, and since Stone House boasts at least fifty rooms in which a pair of females might lose themselves, am I safe in assuming that the new baronet and his wife are not to your liking?"

Alex noticed a decided stiffening of Juliet's back, a posture he had become acquainted with over the years, for she assumed it anytime she was obliged to acknowledge a slight. "As it happens," she said, "*we* are not to *their* liking. Or more to the point, *I* am not."

"The buggers," Alex muttered beneath his breath.

Juliet continued as though she had not heard his crude remark. "Because of the new owners' coldness to me, nothing would appease Lady Feather but to profess a desire to vacate Stone House as quickly as possible."

Knowing Lady Featherstone's love for her home,

Alex bit back another vulgarity, reminding himself that he was no longer among his military comrades and must learn to curb his tongue. As well, he was obliged to quell a desire to approach the narrow-minded baronet and give him the benefit of a few well chosen words. Not that such a confrontation would do Juliet the least good. When a person's bias was fixed, there was little chance of changing his opinion for the better. Alex had learned this indisputable fact not long after Juliet came to live with Sir Titus and Lady Featherstone.

Juliet had been only twelve years old at the time, and her grief over the recent death of her mother was still fresh and understandably painful. Furthermore, though Lady Featherstone had been the deceased's godmother, she was a virtual stranger to the sad little waif who was all knobby elbows and big brown eyes.

It was one thing for her ladyship, childless and with a heart as big as the New Forest itself, to accept the orphaned girl with open arms. It was something else for the villagers to do so. Many of the God-fearing inhabitants of Buckler's Hard were affronted at the inclusion into their daily lives of some nameless gentry's natural daughter. As for the quiet, unassuming little girl whose presence inspired such ill will, she had no means of defending herself against the unkindnesses of an often cruel world.

One person who took instant exception to being obliged to doff his hat to her ladyship's new ward was the baker's oldest boy. Though a lad of sixteen, Zekiel Dobbs took delight in taunting the little girl anytime he found her alone. When his behavior went from mere verbal insults to actually pushing Juliet into a rock-filled ditch where she skinned her hands and sustained a deep gash on one knee, Alex had had enough. Though he was no match for the baker's boy in size, they were of a similar age, so Alex took it upon himself to give the ruffian a lesson in manners.

Their meeting took place the afternoon of the ditch incident, but even though Alex gave as good as he got, drawing the bully's cork in exchange for his own black eye, only that one lad learned anything from the encounter. The remainder of the children turned a cold shoulder to Juliet, excluding her from their play, and when Alex's grandfather forbade him to give any further "lessons" there was nothing more he could do. At least his and Tony's friendship, such as it was, saved the little girl from further bloody knees.

According to snippets of news Alex had received in letters from his grandfather, many of the villagers had learned to appreciate the caring young woman Juliet had become, for during the worst of the war years she began writing letters to the Home Office, the prime minister, anyone who might help in the securing of pensions for elderly parents and war widows from the neighborhood. As well, she saw to it personally that several of the older children of those widows were placed in service in respectable homes. Still, there were always a few people who held themselves too good to associate with her, and if the new baronet and his lady numbered among those few, then no amount of words—no matter how well chosen—would serve to amend their thinking.

Recalling that Juliet was rain-soaked from head to foot, Alex began removing his coat. "Here," he said, "you must be freezing."

"No," she said, "do not." She placed one hand over his to stay his movements, but the moment their fingers touched, she drew back.

"But—"

"No!"

Juliet spoke more emphatically than she had meant to, but in the back of her mind was Hermione Quick's accusation that she and Tony might be carrying on a liaison beneath his grandfather's roof. "It would not do for me to return to the house wearing a gentleman's coat. In fact, I wish you will allow me to precede you by at least a quarter of an hour. With guests in the house, there is always a chance of gossip."

He obviously realized the need for these precautions, for to Juliet's relief he nodded his agreement. "I will watch to see that you reach the pleached walkway safely," he said, "then I will do as you ask and remain here for a quarter hour before making my presence known up at the house."

He said no more, merely opened the entrance door and allowed her to step outside. Just as she turned to leave, however, he caught her hand and raised it to his lips, placing a kiss on her bare skin. "Until we meet again," he said.

To her surprise, Juliet felt something like an electric shock run from that spot where his lips touched her skin all the way up her arm. Not at all certain why she had experienced such a feeling, or why it had left her noticeably breathless, she snatched her hand away. Then, without a word, she lifted her skirts and sped up the carriageway, her footfalls making crunching sounds on the crushed stone.

She was almost to the pleached walk when he yelled something to her. She did not hear the words clearly, and though every rational part of her bid her ignore him, she turned back, her hand cupped around her ear as if that would enable her to catch what he said. "What is it?" she yelled.

Following her example, he cupped his hands around his mouth, as if to help his words carry to her. "I said you may keep the coin I gave you."

*Oh! Would he never be serious!*

Turning her back to him, she hurried up the pleached walk, but long after she was beneath the

# Chapter Three

As soon as Juliet was out of sight, Alex closed the door, shot home the bolt so there would be no more intruders, and took the darkened stairs two at a time. He returned to the attic just as Eisner, his brother's rather stiff-rumped new valet, was lighting the candle beside Geofrey Lansdale's narrow bed. "I gave the captain a sip of water with a drop of laudanum in it, Major, so he is sleeping soundly now. Furthermore, on the chance that he might awaken during the night, I have set food and drink within easy reach. I daresay he will do well enough until morning. Unless, of course, you wish me to return here later tonight."

From his tone, it would appear that Eisner thought himself too elevated a gentleman's gentleman to be tending the sick in an attic room, and Alex wished anew that he had brought Ottway with him. Though he appreciated the necessity of being accompanied by a servant whom no one would recognize, Alex sorely missed the stony-faced Welshman. Ottway had been his batman during the entire eight years of his military service, and other than being just the sort of fellow a soldier wanted beside him in battle, Ottway always seemed to know what was needed in a given situation without having to be told.

His brother's new valet, apparently unaware that his

ersatz employer was less than pleased with the service so far rendered, continued in what must pass for an affable manner in one having such an elevated opinion of his own importance. "As my late employer, His Grace, the Duke of Chawton, often said, the best possible medicine for what ails a gentleman is sleep. 'Eisner,' his grace would say, 'be the condition natural, or be it the result of too much imbibing, modern medicine has found no remedy more efficacious than—' "

"Yes, yes," Alex said, already sick to death of hearing the oft-repeated homilies of a man he was fast coming to think of as the Duke of Chawbacon. "I dare say his grace was in the right of it, so let us leave the captain in the healing arms of Morpheus. In the meantime, since I have it on good authority that my grandfather is becoming anxious about my late arrival, I wish you will bring the curricle from its hiding place behind the cottage so that we may continue up the carriageway."

Eisner bowed rather stiffly. "As you wish, Major."

"And, Eisner," Alex called before the servant disappeared down the stairs. "As this ruse is the brainchild of your new employer, I doubt he would be pleased to discover that you had ruined the thing by calling me by the wrong name. I should think 'Mr. Portman' would not be too difficult for you to remember, since that is my brother's name as well. But if you find the name beyond your mental capabilities, please content yourself with a respectful 'sir.' "

The rawest of recruits could have told the valet that the Major's suggestion, though softly spoken, contained an underlying order as unignorable as a cast-iron hammer. As it happened, Eisner needed no such advice. Obviously perceiving the error of his way, the gentleman's gentleman wisely bowed again, this time with a deference he might have shown his late, lamented employer, the duke. "It shall be as you wish, sir."

\*    \*    \*

Juliet, trusting Tony to keep his word about waiting the requested quarter hour, went around to the rear of the house, where she made use of the door leading to the kitchen garden. After slipping inside the house unnoticed, she sped up the servants' stairs to the second floor, then hurried to her bedchamber, a pretty yellow apartment that had once belonged to the twins' mother. Lady Feather was in the adjoining apartment, which had belonged to Lord Bevin's only son. It was a mark of distinction that those particular rooms in the family wing had been set aside for the ladies from Stone House, and had Mrs. Quick known of the circumstances, the old she-cat might not have been so hasty in her wish to be spared Juliet's "low" company.

Not that the shrew's opinion—good or bad—truly mattered to Juliet. All that concerned her at the moment was getting out of her wet clothes before someone saw her and began asking embarrassing questions about where she had been and how she came to be soaked to the skin.

One of the people she would most have liked to avoid was her maid, Morag Browne. Unfortunately, there was little chance of that, for to protect her mistress's reputation against even the slightest slur, Morag insisted upon sleeping on a cot in the dressing room. The instant Juliet opened the bedchamber door, she spied the Scotswoman sitting beside the fireplace mending a tear in the hem of Juliet's riding habit.

At sight of her bedraggled mistress, the unflappable servant set aside the mending and went to the dresser for a towel. "Ach, and did I not send you belowstairs half an hour hence, presentably dressed and ready to take your place at his lordship's dinner table?"

"You did, but—"

"Then how is it, I'd like to know, that you've returned looking for all the world like you'd fallen down a well?"

Juliet knew better than to try to put Morag off with some Banbury tale. The plump little woman, who always wore gray—a fact, along with her erect carriage, that contributed to her resemblance to a pouter pigeon—had been her mother's nursemaid. Morag, along with Lady Feather, constituted Juliet's family, and she both loved and respected the bossy woman. "I went for a walk."

"That much a blind man could see, you being all but drowned. What I want to know is why you chose to go walking about with it coming on to rain."

In hopes of making a long story short, Juliet came right to the point. "When I went belowstairs, the Quick ladies were the only occupants of the music room. They may or may not have known I was within hearing, but in any event I did not care for the turn of their conversation. Especially since its focus was me and my parentage."

"They never! Why, the mean-spirited she-devils," said the staunch Presbyterian. "May the lot of them roast in hell."

Juliet had heard similar animadversions many times during her twenty-six years, and she had learned not to enter into the conversations, but to let Morag express her anger as she saw fit. She more than expressed it now by wrapping a towel around Juliet's wet hair and drying the dusky locks with a fervor that threatened to leave her mistress bald. Thankfully, Morag's fury ran its course before anything too dire occurred.

After tossing the towel aside, the feisty little pouter pigeon turned Juliet around none too gently and began removing the pale pink dinner dress that was now ruined. "Now that we know what we're up against, luv, I see this frock was all wrong. Too demure by half. Better for you to face those she-devils wearing something a bit more sophisticated."

"If you are girding me up for war, Morag, what say you to the apple-green sarcenet?"

"A good choice, for 'tis beautiful you look in green. And you'll wear me own cashmere shawl, I'm thinking, the one your sainted mother gave me. The red and green tartan will show them so-called ladies that they must keep a civil tongue in their heads. If not, they'll incur the wrath of one whose bloodline includes many a painted-faced Scots warrior."

Juliet agreed to wear the shawl, but as it turned out, she had no need of the tartan talisman. By the time she slipped quietly into the handsome blue and cream music room, with its elegant fleur-de-lis-patterned carpet, the attention of the entire assembled party was on the newest arrival, Lord Bevin's heir, who stood tall and impressive in his beautifully cut evening clothes.

"Such a pleasure to see you again, Anthony," Lady Feather said.

"The pleasure is all mine," he replied, "for you must know, Lady Featherstone, that you were my first love."

Her ladyship laughed. "Such unconscionable flummery, sir." Though a touch of genuine color tinged her powdered and rouged cheeks, she gave Tony's shoulder a firm tap with her fan to show she was not fooled by his flattery, then stepped aside to allow him to greet the other guests.

"My boy," Lord Bevin said, "you know Claude Quick, for he and I have been friends for years, but I am not certain you are acquainted with his lovely wife."

"Mrs. Quick," Tony said.

It was while he bowed over the middle-aged she-cat's hand that Juliet noticed for the first time the way the candlelight reflected off his sun-streaked brown hair.

*Sun-streaked hair?*

"So pleased to meet you at last," Mrs. Quick simpered. "Pray allow me, sir, to make you known to my daughters." Motioning for the young ladies to come forward, she said, "This is my eldest, Beatrice, and my youngest, Celeste."

"Miss Quick, Miss Celeste," he said, "I hope your journey from town was not too taxing."

The two young ladies curtsied, and Tony bowed politely. With his right leg forward, he bent at the waist in a very elegant manner, and as he did so Juliet could not help but notice how the muscles in his back flexed and bunched beneath the snug burgundy coat.

*Muscles? Tony? And when had he developed such broad shoulders?*

Not half an hour hence, she had been captured by a surprisingly strong arm and pulled against a rock-hard chest, yet at the time she had not given the matter serious thought. Now she wondered how she could have overlooked such manly attributes. She saw Tony Portman several times a year; how could she not have noticed that he positively exuded health?

Lady Featherstone, realizing that Juliet stood near the door, called to her. "Come, my dear, and help us welcome this bad boy, who is late as usual."

"Of course, Lady Feather, though I am not certain it is I who should welcome him. After all, this is his home and I am merely a guest."

"Come then," Tony said, turning to smile at her, his hands outstretched, "join us by the fire, and let a friend of long standing welcome you to Portman Park."

Though embarrassed by the knowledge that all eyes were on her, Juliet crossed the room and placed her hands in his. The instant their fingers met, she realized why she had reacted so strangely at the cottage when she had touched him. These were not Tony's hands. Tony never rode without his gloves, and his hands, like those of most gentlemen, were soft and smooth, his grip often carelessly loose. The hands that held hers now, the grip firm and strong, were work-roughened and quite brown from exposure to the sun.

The face, too, now that she saw it in the light from at least a dozen candles, was unfashionably tanned. And Tony Portman was nothing if not fashionable!

Instantly Juliet glanced away, for a preposterous thought had begun to niggle at her brain. Tony, like the celebrated poet, Lord Byron, prided himself on his pallor: he thought it lent him a romantic air.

Unable to stop herself, Juliet looked up, but even before she allowed her gaze to travel from his stubborn jawline, past his far-from-perfect nose to his blue-gray eyes, she knew what she would find. She knew the true identity of the man before her, and judging by the devilish twinkle in his eye, he knew the exact moment she realized that he was, in fact, Major Alexander Portman, and not his twin.

In the dimness of Auntie's Cottage, she had mistaken him for Tony for the simple reason that it was Tony she had been expecting. The heir to the Park, Tony was obliged by his grandfather to come home every few weeks for updates on the business of the estate. For that reason, his presence on the property was nothing remarkable.

As for Alex, he had not been home to Hampshire in more than two years, and as far as Juliet knew he was not expected here anytime soon. When he was last at Portman Park, it was for a short stay, and Juliet had been away the entire time taking part in the wedding of a school friend. As a result, she had not seen Alex in nearly four years, and even then she had seen him only from a distance. He had not seen her. She had eaten something that caused her to break out in hives, and because of her pride she had refused to go over to Portman Park with her face covered in welts.

Those rare encounters notwithstanding, Juliet was

surprised that she had been fooled, for she had never had any difficulty distinguishing one twin from the other.

She always knew when she was with Alex. Why should she not, when just the sight of him was enough to make her heart threaten to jump right out of her chest? It had been that way for as long as she could remember, even before that spring day when he fought the baker's boy for her. On that day, however, Alex became her hero for life.

The twins were nearing sixteen when Juliet first met them. The school term was not yet over, but Alex and Tony had been sent down from Eton for a fortnight because their latest escapade had gone beyond the bounds of a childish prank. One of them—no one knew which one—had flouted the school's curfew rules. After stuffing pillows beneath the bedcovers in a manner that made them resemble a sleeping boy, one of the twins, along with another student, had sneaked down to the local pub. When they returned later that evening, more than a little inebriated, the bagwig was waiting for them. The guilty boys were ordered to present themselves one at a time the following morning for a caning.

When morning came, both Alex and Tony reported to the headmaster's rooms. Because that confused gentleman could not determine which of the twins had earned the caning, he sent them both home so their grandfather could see they were properly chastised.

Juliet never did learn the full story, though from the way Alex's face reddened when she asked which twin had actually committed the offense, she suspected that for once Tony was innocent of wrongdoing. Not that it mattered to Juliet; all she knew was that in her entire twelve years she had never met anyone like the twins. To her, they were positively godlike. They were handsome, fun-loving, and daring enough to try anything, while she was quiet, and too shy to do more than speak when spoken to.

It was probably her shyness that led the baker's boy to believe he could get away with bullying her. Always before Zekiel Dobbs had been content to call her names, but that particular day, when he discovered her alone in the lane just beyond Stone House, something about her refusal to react to his taunts seemed to infuriate him. She had climbed into a rock-filled ditch to pick a bouquet of wildflowers for Morag, who was laid low with a toothache, and when she climbed out of the ditch, Zekiel spread wide his long arms and would not let her step into the lane.

"Ye don't belong here," he said, his moon-shaped face made even homelier by the hate he clearly felt no need to hide. "Any but a idjet would have figured it out by now that we don't want no bastards here in Buckler's Hard. Go back where ye came from. Go back to the slut what whelped ye."

*Slut!*

Juliet had been called a bastard before, and each time she had done exactly what Morag had told her to do, she had pretended not to hear the vile remark. But this time was different. This time a foul-mouthed, ignorant lout had insulted her mother—the sweet, gentle woman Juliet loved above all others—and Juliet refused to pretend she had not heard. Some things just could not be ignored.

Before the cretin suspected what she meant to do, Juliet dropped the bouquet, then reached out and scraped her fingernails down the length of his dirty forearm, making him draw back in pain and surprise. "Ye've drawn blood, you ugly little mongrel!"

He said nothing more, but Juliet knew from the way Zekiel's upper lip curled into a snarl that she was about to pay for her defiance.

A well-behaved little girl, she had never experi-

enced anything more than a gentle verbal reprimand
from her mother or Morag, but she had seen enough
village boys involved in fisticuffs to know what they
were capable of. Frightened into immobility, she
watched in horror as the angry Zekiel drew back his
fist, then hit her full-force in her midsection. The blow
was both harder and more painful than she could have
imagined, and it sent her flying into the rock-filled
ditch, where she lay for what seemed forever, strug-
gling to draw breath into lungs that felt as if they were
on fire.

While tears of pain and mortification streamed
down Juliet's face, Zekiel continued to yell insults at
her. After a time, however, he must have exhausted
his supply of crude words, for he turned and walked
away, for all the world as if nothing of any real importance had occurred.

Only after the lout was out of sight did Juliet feel
safe in climbing back up to the lane. She hurt all over,
but the only injuries immediately visible were on her
palms, which were scraped and dirty, and on one knee,
which bled from a deep gash.

Too embarrassed to go back to Stone House and
tell them what had happened, she tore a flounce from
the end of her cotton shift and was attempting to
stanch the flow of blood when Alex came by. He had
been to the riverbank, and he carried a fishing rod in
one hand and an old woven-willow creel in the other.
When he spied Juliet standing there, her skin dirty
and blood-smeared and her face streaked with tears,
he dropped both the rod and the creel and ran to her.
"Good God, little one, how came you to be hurt?"

"I . . . I . . ."

As if discerning what had happened, Alex muttered
an oath she had never heard before. "Did you fall?"
he asked, his teeth clenched so hard she could barely
understand his words, "or did someone do this to
you?"

It never occurred to Juliet to dissemble, so she told him the truth—all except for the name-calling. She could not bring herself to repeat the insulting words the bully had called her, not to this godlike creature.

Her brief story finished, she raised her arm, using her sleeve in an attempt to wipe away her tears. To her surprise, Alex moved her arm away; then caught her by the shoulders, obliging her to look up at him. At that moment, his eyes, which she had always thought remarkably handsome, resembled hard, cold marble. "This is very important, Juliet. Are you certain it was the baker's son, and not some other lad who hit you? Someone younger and more your size?"

"I am certain."

"But Zeke Dobbs is at least my age, surely he knows better than to—"

"It was him."

"*Merde!* That damned, stupid pig, I'll—" Biting off the remainder of his words, Alex took a clean linen handkerchief from his pocket and gently dabbed at Juliet's tear-streaked cheeks. Juliet stood quite still, mesmerized by his attention. If her life had depended upon it, she could not have said which had left her more breathless, the hard blow Zekiel Dobbs had dealt her midsection, or the tender way Alex Portman dried her tears.

His task completed, Alex handed the cloth to her and told her to hold it against the gash on her knee. Though Juliet hated to ruin the linen square, nothing would have induced her to refuse Alex's offer.

"Wait here," he said, "until I return."

He had gone only a few yards down the lane when he suddenly stopped and turned back, pointing to the rod and creel, which still lay where he had dropped them. "Do not let anyone touch that creel, for I have caught what is surely the largest salmon ever seen in Hampshire. It's a beauty," he added, "and I mean to have it mounted."

Not the least insulted to be asked to guard a fish, Juliet did just as he asked, ready to defend his prized catch with her life if need be. Fortunately, it did not come to that, for in the half hour or so that Alex was gone, not one soul traveled the lane.

When he returned, limping slightly, it was obvious that he had been in a fight. His hair was disheveled and wet with sweat, and his clothes were covered in dirt and grass stains, as though he had been rolling around on the ground. Worse yet, his left eye was red-ringed and nearly swollen shut.

"Oh, Alex. You are injured!"

He shrugged off her concern. "I drew Zeke's cork," he said, proudly displaying a smear of blood on the knuckles of his right hand. "And you needn't fear a repeat of today's assault, for I told Zeke there was more where that came from if he even thought about bothering you again."

It was all Juliet could do to remain still, when what she wanted to do was throw her arms around Alex's neck and squeeze him with all her might. Of course, she was much too shy to do anything of that nature, so she merely held his handkerchief out to him. "Here," she said, "my knee is all better."

"That's all right," he said, eying the bloody square, "you may have it."

"Oh, thank you," she said, her voice little more than an awed whisper. "I shall keep it always."

When she returned to Stone House, she washed that linen square until it was once again snowy white, and then when it was dry she folded it very neatly and placed it in the little velvet-lined jewelry box that held her mother's cameo and gold locket. The handkerchief deserved to be with Juliet's other treasures, for it was a gift from a hero. From her hero.

It was not to be wondered at that she fell in love with Alex that day. She was only twelve years old, but she gave him her heart, and the gift was irrevocable. Not that she ever told him how she felt. He did not know. And he never would.

What would be the point?

No one had to tell her what sort of wives Lord Bevin expected his grandsons to bring home. Juliet knew as well as the twins what was due their name, and an alliance with someone's natural daughter was out of the question.

"I have a perfectly valid reason for being in the cottage," Alex whispered, bringing Juliet's thoughts back to the present. "Will you remain silent regarding our earlier meeting until we can discuss it privately?"

He had leaned close, so only she could hear his softly spoken words, but with everyone in the music room watching them, the last thing Juliet wanted was for it to appear that she and "the heir" were sharing a private conversation.

The twinkle of amusement was gone from Alex's eyes, and in its place was an unspoken plea for Juliet not to expose him. The plea was unnecessary, of course, for she would never betray him.

He must have read her answer in her eyes, for he smiled. "Later," he said.

# Chapter Four

As it happened, "later" stretched into the small hours, and it was past midnight before Alex found himself outside Juliet's bedchamber, scratching lightly at her door. The evening had seemed interminable, for after the ritual glasses of sherry had been drunk in the music room, there was the long and very formal dinner to be gotten through. Following that, of course, was the unavoidable musical program, whose challenge—Alex could call it nothing less—had been issued at table between the fish course and the dessert.

At first, the meal had gone well enough, for the food was delicious, and the lovely rosewood table that had stood in the Portman Park dining room for more than three hundred years was beautifully set with Irish linens and the cobalt-and-gold dinnerware that had been a wedding gift to the twins' mother. Nothing could have been more convivial, for while dish after dish of elegantly prepared foods was offered to Lord Bevin and his guests, the two dozen candles that burned in the Italian-crystal chandelier caused prisms of color to dance off the wine glasses.

"To old friends," his lordship said, raising his glass to Lady Feather, "and to my honored guests."

"Hear, hear," everyone replied, lifting their glasses

in salute, then sipping the aged French wine the six liveried footmen stood waiting to replenish.

To Alex's surprise, Juliet added very little to the overall conversation. He might have been misled into believing her lack of loquaciousness had something to do with what had occurred between them at the cottage, had he not seen firsthand the coolness with which Mrs. Quick treated any remark from Juliet, and how little her dinner partners responded to her few, yet polite, offerings.

Mr. Claude Quick was her partner to her left, and while that gentleman contented himself with downing glass after glass of his host's excellent wine, Miss Celeste Quick, Juliet's partner to her right, responded to all questions with monosyllables. In fact, that young lady scarcely lifted her gaze from her plate, giving the majority of her concentration to pushing small, flaky bites of halibut *en brochette* around her plate.

Not that Alex faulted the pretty blonde, whose face had grown steadily pinker until it resembled the strawberry aspic she had not yet tasted. She was embarrassed, and rightly so, for from the moment they had taken their places at table, her mother—to whom subtlety was clearly a foreign word—had begun in earnest an attempt to ensnare "Tony's" interest.

"Dear Mr. Portman," the harpy began almost every sentence, to insure his full regard. Because the woman sat to his immediate left, there was nothing Alex could do but give her his full attention.

What followed the initial claiming of his notice was a recitation of the many charms of her daughters, in case "the heir" had failed to observe them on his own. Then, as if these heavy-handed tactics were not enough, she continued with a list of each girl's various accomplishments. "And," she said, at last bringing the cataloguing to an end, "both my angels are gifted at the pianoforte."

"Is that an unbiased evaluation, ma'am, or must one make allowances for a mother's understandable partiality?"

For a moment, it looked as if the woman might take exception to his remark, but apparently thinking better of it, she chose to smile and wag a finger at him, as though he were a naughty boy. "My dear Mr. Portman, you are a caution. I had heard that you were a notorious tease, and now I see that the reports were accurate."

"Another unbiased evaluation? I must say, ma'am, you are uncommonly kind. Though for the life of me I cannot imagine why you are disposed to be so charitable to me."

That blatant remark bordered on rudeness, and Alex was not surprised when Juliet choked on a sip of wine and his grandfather gave him a warning frown.

Mrs. Quick merely blinked at him, as if not sure what to make of that last comment. Nothing if not determined, she chose once again not to take offense and returned to the subject of her daughters' musical ability. "As you say, sir, I am partial, but forgivably so I believe, for both Beatrice and Celeste had the benefit of instruction from Signor Parlotti. As I am certain you know, being invited to all the *ton* parties as you are, the signor is the most sought-after performer in Europe."

Since Alex had not the least idea who Signor Parlotti might be, he kept his reply as innocuous as possible. "I am constantly amazed, ma'am, at the accomplishments of today's young ladies. Each one seems more talented than the last."

"Perhaps," Lord Bevin said, "one or both of the Misses Quick will favor us with a selection or two following dinner."

"And if we are very good," Alex added, "perhaps Juliet will favor us with a song as well."

Mrs. Quick, clearly less than pleased to have the future musical display include someone other than her daughters, looked directly across the table. Fortunately, before she could address Juliet, Miss Celeste offered her unsolicited mite to the conversation.

"Do you sing, Miss Moseby?"

"Yes, I do. A little."

"Then I pray you, do not let my sister and me be the only performers."

If looks could sear, poor Miss Celeste would have been consumed by flames, for the stare the young lady received from her "doting" mother was heated by her outrage.

When Mrs. Quick spoke, however, it was not to her daughter but to Juliet, and her tone was so condescending she might have been speaking to a servant only just released from the workhouse. "My daughters," she said, "sing in both French and Italian. As an orphan, Miss Moseby, I daresay you were not given the benefit of any very superior musical instruction. A shame really, for it is most important that a female embrace such refinements. One can always tell a lady by her proficiency in music, art, and foreign tongues."

Lady Featherstone, usually the kindest of beings, had sat quietly during most of the exchange, but she took exception to this obvious insult aimed at her ward. "I will have you know, madam, that Juliet is a most accomplished musician. And," she added, like one delivering a telling blow, "as you will see for yourself later, she is proficient in French, Italian, *and* German."

Clearly, the daggers were drawn!

"As for art," Lady Featherstone continued, "it might interest you to know that when Juliet was at Miss Trillium's Female Academy in Brighton, her watercolors were framed and displayed with pride throughout the school, where they were much admired by visiting parents."

"Oh," Mrs. Quick replied, "you went to school, did you, Miss Moseby? I had no idea. You can read, then?"

Not surprisingly, this last question elicited a gasp from Lady Featherstone. "Madam, I will thank you to—"

"Lady Feather," Juliet interrupted quickly, "surely it is time and more that we left the gentlemen to their port."

Recalled to her duties as hostess, Lady Featherstone set her napkin beside her plate, then rose. "Lord Bevin. Gentlemen. If you will excuse us now, we will be pleased to have you join us later in the music room."

Naturally, the gentlemen stood as well, assuring her ladyship that they would not linger over their port. Which they did not. After their guest had tossed back his second glass of the sweet, fortified wine—an act that was as swift as it was silent—Lord Bevin nodded to his grandson, whose glass had not been touched, then suggested they not delay in joining the ladies.

As Alex feared, when he and his grandfather, along with Mr. Claude Quick, entered the music room, there was a decided chill in the air. The two older ladies, like duelists with their seconds, sat at opposite ends of the room, with the fleur-de-lis carpet apparently a barrier not to be crossed by either set of combatants. Needless to say, the musical dueling that followed, though bloodless, was as fiercely fought as any meeting of honor ever held at Lincoln's Inn, Holborn.

It is possible that Mr. Claude Quick enjoyed the music that followed. Of course, by that time the gentleman was so jug-bitten that he fell asleep in the blue damask wing chair closest to the hearth, totally oblivious to the duel being fought between his wife and his hostess. As far as Alex could determine, however, he, his grandfather, and all three of the young ladies fervently wished themselves elsewhere.

Some time around ten, the butler brought in the tea tray, putting an end to the musicale. Shortly thereafter, having partaken of only one duty cup, Lord Bevin declared himself desirous of a few moments alone with his grandson and begged his guests to excuse them. Like a pair of cowards, the Portman gentlemen made good their escape, comfortable in the knowledge that one of the servants would let them know if any bodies were left lying about on the carpet.

What happened after they quit the room, Alex was never to know, but he was more than happy to spend a few quiet moments with his grandfather beside the old gentleman's bedchamber fire; especially since he had not seen his grandfather for two years. Naturally, he would have enjoyed their coze far more had he not been pretending to be his brother. Even so, he took the opportunity to ask his grandfather a few broad questions about estate management, a circumstance that delighted the old gentleman out of all proportion to the importance of the questions.

When the small ormolu clock on the mantel chimed midnight, Alex begged his grandfather's forgiveness for keeping him from his bed for so long. "No doubt you have been wishing me gone this hour and more."

"Not at all, my boy." He gave "Tony's" shoulder an affectionate squeeze. "I have enjoyed our talk more than I can say, and with this new interest you have shown, I feel confident that you will make an excellent master one day."

"Thank you, Grandfather. From you, that is praise indeed."

Alex left the old gentleman in the capable hands of his valet, then went to his own—or rather, Tony's—bedchamber, where Eisner waited to help him prepare for bed. "Just get me out of this damned snug coat," Alex said, "then take yourself off to bed."

"But, sir, I—"

"Now."

Without further argument, the valet did as he was bid. He helped Alex work himself free of his brother's evening coat, which had restricted his movement mercilessly, then he bowed and took himself off to his own bedchamber.

Only after Alex was alone was he able to breathe freely. He removed the cream waistcoat, unwound the heavily starched neckcloth, and with a muttered oath tossed them both on a nearby chair, wishing as he did so that he could as easily rid himself of this foolish impersonation. "Tony, Tony," he said, "what have you gotten me into? If you were here at this moment, I would gladly strangle you with your own cravat."

Recalling his promise to explain his actions in the cottage to Juliet, and hopeful that she might agree to help him shield Geofrey Lansdale from discovery, Alex lit a single candle from the brace left on the table beside the large, carved oak bed. Wearing only his white linen shirt and the satin knee breeches that were de rigueur for any gentleman dining at Portman Park, he moved quietly down the darkened corridor toward the pretty yellow suite that had once belonged to his mother.

Only as he scratched at the door to the suite did it occur to him that this might not be a good idea. Juliet was no longer a little girl—she was a grown woman, as his cavalier exploration of her in the cottage had revealed all too clearly—and though they had been friends for donkey's years, the time had passed when he could seek her out at any time without caring a fig for the proprieties.

Realizing the folly of this late-night visit, he turned to retrace his steps, but as he did so, he heard the creak of the hinges as the door was opened. From the surprised look on Juliet's face when she realized who held the candle aloft, it was clear that she had not taken his reference to "later" to mean the middle of the night.

On the instant, surprise turned to concern. "Alex? Is something amiss? Lord Bevin? Is he ill?"

"Shh," he said, his finger across his lips. "Nothing is wrong except my sense of timing."

She blinked, obviously confused. "Then I do not understand—"

"Of course you do not. Pray, forgive me for alarming you needlessly. My grandfather is in excellent health, save for the obvious affliction of having a grandson who is an ass."

At least she could still smile. " 'Tis a most regrettable affliction to be sure. Especially when one considers that his lordship has two such grandsons."

"Witch! Leave it to you to belabor the obvious."

She took no offense, merely reached to her right shoulder where a thick braid lay half finished, and with swift, deft fingers began to plait the strands, not even bothering to look at what she was doing. "Alex, are you foxed?"

"Not at present, but I plan to remedy that situation the moment I return to my bedchamber."

He watched her finish the braid and wondered, fleetingly, if she tied the ends with a ribbon, as she had done when she was a child. Whatever she used, she did not have the item with her, so she contented herself with holding the unsecured ends in her right hand so they did not come undone once again.

Alex had always liked her hair. She had been a rather funny-looking child—with her pointy chin and her serious eyes—but even then she'd had really pretty hair, which she always wore confined in two plaits. The style suited her, as did the color, an unpre-

tentious brown, reminiscent of chocolate with cream
stirred in. But it was the texture Alex admired, for
it was as shiny as satin and as soft as the fur of a
new kitten.

Once, when she was quite young, he had taken hold
of a lock that had come loose and rubbed it between
his fingers. He had never forgotten the feel of it.

Realizing that he was staring at her like some young
looby who had never seen a female *en dishabille,* he
bowed and said, "Pray, forgive me for waking you."

"I was not asleep. In fact, I was reading by the
fire." She pointed toward the adjoining dressing room,
where the door was ajar. "How could anyone sleep
with that going on?"

For the first time, Alex noticed the unmistakable
sound of snoring. "Morag?" he asked.

"Who else?"

"So, the indomitable Scotswoman still sleeps nearby
to protect your reputation? Such loyalty is commendable."

"Commendable, yes. Restful, no."

Alex could not suppress a chuckle. "It does sound
a bit like a battalion of soldiers on the march. Enemy
soldiers, of course."

"Oh, of course, and when you heard them, you
came to rescue me. How gallant."

"Gallantry," he said, "is my middle name."

"Unfortunately, your first and second names are
*abominable* and *coward.* Were it not so, you would
have rescued me from that fiasco in the music room.
Instead, you sneaked away without so much as a
glance in my direction."

He did not bother to deny the accusation. "By the
way, who won the duel?"

She shrugged her shoulders. "Who can say? In any
event, Lady Feather has declared it to be her mission
in life to see that you—that is to say, Tony—is not

allowed to fall into the clutches of that harpy and her daughters."

"I daresay my brother will be appreciative of her ladyship's help, for he has no wish to be leg-shackled at this time."

"Is that why Tony is among the missing? So that he may avoid—"

"Deuce take it! Of all the stupid—" A sudden and rather painful blob of hot wax had fallen onto Alex's wrist, and he was obliged to swallow the swear word he had been about to utter.

Like a fool, he had forgotten about the candle in his hand, and he had ceased to hold it at an angle. As a result of his carelessness, his wrist had been splattered by the dripping wax. He quickly changed the candle from his left to his right hand, so he could examined the spot where the hot wax had landed, but to his surprise, Juliet was even quicker. Without a word, she reached out and carefully folded back the end of his shirt sleeve so she could examine the burn herself. Her immediate reaction was an indrawn breath. "Oh, Alex. That must hurt something fierce."

For a career soldier with a number of battle scars on his body, a bit of hot wax was a momentary distraction, of no more consequence to Alex than the sting of a bee. Before he could explain that fact to Juliet, however, she cradled his wrist in both her hands, then bent down and began to blow softly on the spot.

"Give me a moment to cool the wax," she said. "When it hardens, I will remove it as gently as possible, so that I can ascertain the degree of the burn."

With her head bent, the thick braid she had been holding fell forward, and Alex watched as the ends unravelled, spinning like a whirling dervish. Apparently Juliet was far more concerned about his wound than about her hair, for she ignored the loosened tresses, not caring in the least that they brushed against Alex's arm.

Unfortunately, the same could not be said for Alex.

This was the first time in years he had seen Juliet's hair in any way other than in the neat, twisty sort of bun she wore at the nape of her neck, and he found himself fighting an almost irresistible urge to reach out and continue to loosen the tresses, so he could run his fingers through their silken length.

*Whoa! Where had that idea come from?*

Perhaps it was floating on the air, like that hint of lilacs that seemed to come from Juliet's unbound tresses. It was a delicate aroma, yet it filled his nostrils, teasing his senses and making him long to lean closer for a better—

*Damnation!* Obviously some evil genie had taken possession of his mind; otherwise, he would not be having these thoughts. Not for the first time, he wished he had remained in his bedchamber, instead of stealing down the corridor to Juliet's.

And he wished to hell she would stop blowing her warm breath on his skin! He was only a man, after all, and clearly he was far too susceptible to temptation.

Not three minutes ago, in those moments before she had opened her bedchamber door, Alex had reminded himself that Juliet was no longer a girl. Now, as she held his wrist, her soft breath caressing his far-too-sensitive skin, he had to remind himself that he was supposed to be a gentleman.

To his infinite relief, she finally stopped tormenting him with her soft breath. She straightened and tossed that thick fall of hair back over her shoulder, and he was congratulating himself on not having given in to temptation, when she tested his strength even further. With a gentleness that was almost his undoing, she began to circle the burned spot with her fingertips, the movement slow and maddeningly tantalizing. "This should help," she said.

*Help what!*

"Just give it a few more moments," she said, "for the wax is almost cool."

*Ha! That was all she knew!* Nothing on his body was cool. In fact, if she continued that soft stroking of his wrist, the blasted wax would soon melt and run off of its own accord.

Alex's sanity was deserting him by leaps and bounds, for he had begun to imagine other places where he wished she would employ those magic fingers. In an attempt to hang on to what willpower he still possessed, he averted his gaze from those mesmerizing circles and looked instead at her—really looked at her—from her head down to her toes and back.

Her feet were encased in practical carpet slippers, and from beneath the hem of the green flannel dressing gown that was as utilitarian as it was unprovocative there peeped an equally utilitarian flannel nightgown. All in all, she looked like what she was, a grown-up version of the serious little girl she had once been. And yet, as Alex studied her, she looked up at him with her big brown eyes, and every pulse point in his body sprang to life.

"Come inside," she said, giving his hand a gentle tug.

"What!"

"I want to put some ointment and a sticking plaster on that burn."

*Sticking plaster!* Great Caesar's ghost! Of the two dozen totally inappropriate ideas that had burst full-blown into his mind following that invitation to come inside, not one had involved a sticking plaster.

He tried in vain to think of something to say—something that would explain why he could not, under any circumstances, put one foot inside her bedchamber. When nothing came to him, he took the coward's route and merely turned on his heels and walked away. Juliet probably thought him insane, but if he did not get away from her that very instant, he might well do something they would both regret.

It was only later, while he paced the floor, wearing a rut into the finely woven Axminster carpet that adorned his brother's bedchamber, trying to forget Juliet's touch and the way her warm breath had whispered across his senses, that Alex remembered something his overheated brain had forgotten earlier. Morag Browne. Morag, the faithful watchdog who made it her life's work to guard Juliet's reputation, had been asleep in the dressing room, her door ajar.

The servant had been there all along. If Alex had done as Juliet asked and gone into her bedchamber, the instant his foot touched the carpet, Morag would have been beside him, fully awake and probably supplying the ointment and sticking plaster. With her chaperon so close at hand, no wonder Juliet had felt free to stand in the doorway talking with him.

Alex had been right earlier when he said his grandfather had an ass for a grandson. What a fool he had been to allow his baser nature to misconstrue the entire encounter outside Juliet's door. Even when she invited him into her bedchamber, she was not being provocative, she was just being a Good Samaritan. The fault was entirely his, and it served him right that he could not get her out of his mind—she who was probably tucked up in her bed this very moment, sleeping the sleep of the innocent, while he paced back and forth, a mass of awakened senses and throbbing body parts.

And blast it all! He had forgotten the reason he went to talk to Juliet in the first place, to ask her to trust him and to stay away from the cottage!

The way Alex's luck was going, before he could

explain to her the need for secrecy, Juliet would discover Geofrey Lansdale for herself. And when she did, chances were she would set up a hue and cry that would be heard all the way to London.

# Chapter Five

About one thing, at least, Alex had been correct: Juliet did discover Geofrey Lansdale the very next morning, though she did not set up a hue and cry. In expecting such a reaction from her, Alex had been way off the mark; just as he had erred when he pictured her last night tucked up in her bed, sleeping the sleep of the innocent.

In truth, Juliet had lain awake half the night, replaying those minutes when she and Alex had stood at her door, his strong wrist in her hands. She had meant only to do what she could to relieve the pain of the burn, but the instant she touched his skin—felt the strong bones beneath and the fine, soft hairs above—she had been filled with such pleasure that she had not wanted the sensation to end.

Later, of course, the heat of embarrassment had seared her face, for she knew she had behaved wantonly. Alex was injured, undoubtedly in pain, and all she could think about was the thrill it gave her letting her fingertips circle his wound. Circle after mesmerizing circle, simply because if felt so good to her.

Not that the fault was all hers!

She was willing to accept the blame when it was rightly hers, but scratching at her bedchamber door was Alex's doing. That bit of culpability was his alone, and she would tell him so if the subject ever came up. Not that she expected it to.

Naturally, she had not expected to open her door and find Alex standing there, the light from a single candle casting shadows on the hard planes of his face and the strong column of his throat. And if it came down to it, she was not above reminding him that a gentleman would not have come to her in his shirt-sleeves, with the neck of the linen open so that a person could not help but admire the expanse of manly chest revealed.

Did he think women were made of stone?

Surely not, for there had been a moment there, when she had asked him to come inside so she could put some ointment on his wound, that Juliet had felt an intense current pass between them. There had been a flash of passion in Alex's eyes, she was certain of it, and just the memory of that look sent heat coursing through her body.

But then, what did she know of passion? She, a twenty-six-year-old spinster. She knew what it was to love, for she had loved Alex Portman for as long as she could remember, but passion required two people. Two who loved and were loved in return. And Alex did not love her.

How could he? She was Miss Serious. More than that, she was someone's natural daughter, and no matter how hard she tried to forget that fact, it was always there, influencing every facet of her life.

"It should not matter," she whispered into the darkness. "I am me, Juliet, and if someone truly loved me—" She did not finish the sentence, for the futility of it filled her heart with a sadness that nearly choked her. Though she had not cried in years, she turned her face into her pillow, where Morag would not hear her, and she wept.

Eventually she must have cried herself to sleep, for

when she awoke several hours later, her head felt as though it were stuffed with cotton wool. Darkness had not completely vanished from the sky, but the stars were gone, leaving in their absence the pale, soft light of the slowly bluing sky.

Knowing what she needed to do to clear away the cobwebs in her head, if not the sadness in her heart, Juliet dressed quietly, so as not to disturb Morag. After fastening a warm blue woolen cloak at her neck, then pulling the hood up over her head, she hurried down the stone steps and through the vestibule. Once outside, she breathed deeply, filling her lungs with the fresh, moist air.

Oh, how she missed the pretty little roan mare Sir Titus and Lady Feather had given her on her twenty-fifth birthday. Lord Bevin had said she could bring Princess over to the Park's stables, and once she and Lady Feather moved into Auntie's Cottage, Juliet would do just that. She was accustomed to a solitary morning ride, and after only a few days at the Park, she sorely missed the exercise and the solitude. For now, she would satisfy her need for both with a long walk. If last night's rain had not turned the lane into a quagmire, perhaps she would walk all the way to the river.

As it turned out, she dared not leave the immediate grounds of the Park, for a thick layer of fog hovered just a few feet above the earth. Once she left the pleached walk and stepped out onto the carriageway, even familiar landmarks refused to come into focus. She knew the walled entrance to the estate was out there, but try as she would to peer through the impenetrable grayness, Juliet could not see the stuccoed arch.

A hush hung over everything as well, for apparently there was not a single bird with enough faith in the sun's future appearance to announce the new day. Unlike those winged doubting Thomases, Juliet knew the sun would eventually put in an appearance and burn off the fog, but until that time she was not so foolish as to wander far from the house. As long as she could hear the unmistakable sound of her boots crunching on the crushed stone of the carriageway, she would be in no danger.

She would walk a little way, and if she spied the cottage, which she knew was slightly more than half a mile from the manor house, she would stop in there for that look around she had promised herself the previous evening. If the fog concealed the cottage from view, however, she had only to turn and retrace her steps to the pleached walk.

As it turned out, she had no trouble at all finding the cottage, for the simple reason that a light shone in one of the attic windows. "Alex," she muttered, the word all but swallowed up by the fog, "what are you up to this time?" Not for one moment did she doubt it was him in the front attic room.

Last evening he had promised to explain to her why he had been sneaking about in the darkened cottage when he was expected at the manor house. "Later," he had said. Now, she told herself, was quite late enough, for he'd had time and to spare to concoct whatever Banbury tale he meant to foist upon her. And whatever his story—truth or fiction—she wanted to hear it.

Using that light in the window as her beacon, she made it to the front of the cottage without mishap, though she wished she had had the foresight to wear pattens to protect her boots from the puddles lying in wait for her between the carriageway and the door. Already the cold water was soaking her stockings and freezing her toes.

Lifting the latch, she let herself into the small, quiet vestibule. The hinges of the door squeaked in protest, just as they had the night before, disturbing the silence. This time, however, Juliet had no reason to be concerned about interrupting a lovers' tryst, so as soon as she closed the door behind her, she walked toward the narrow staircase, her hand outstretched, searching for the carved pineapple finial. Once she located the finial, she lifted the hem of her cloak and her dress, then made her way up the uncarpeted stairs, not bothering to stop until she had reached the door to the attic rooms.

As before, she detected the scent of a candle, and even though she knew she would find Alex on the other side of the door, common courtesy demanded that she knock before entering the room. "Fair warning," she called into the stillness. "Here I come, ready or not."

This time the door hinges did not squeak. But Juliet did. Or perhaps she screamed. Of only one thing was she certain, that the man she saw—the man who stared directly at her, his green eyes filled with a combination of fear and reckless determination—was not Alex.

This man lay on one of the servant's cots just inside the low-ceilinged room, and though he wore a nightshirt and had the covers pulled up to his chin, he was not one of the Portman Park servants come for a tryst. He was a complete stranger to Juliet, though she would wager her newest bonnet from Madam Yvette's that he was no stranger to Alex Portman.

Unless she missed her guess, the bandages that swathed the gentleman's head, not to mention the swollen lower lip, had much to do with his being hidden away in one of the attic rooms of Auntie's Cottage. And his being here was the reason Alex had been tiptoeing around yesterday, making sure that no one got too close to the attic.

Finding her voice at last, Juliet begged the man's pardon for intruding. "I . . . I expected to find Alex Portman here."

Suddenly realizing how that sounded, a woman meeting a man in this empty house, Juliet blushed hotly. "That is to say, I did not *expect* to find him, we had no appointment or anything of that nature, but when I saw the light I naturally assumed . . ."

"That it was Alex," the gentleman offered when she said no more.

From the wary expression in his eyes, it was obvious that he was as surprised to see her as she was to discover him. No, he was more than surprised, he was suspicious, and it occurred to Juliet that the chill in the air might not be the only reason his right arm was concealed beneath the rough blanket.

Smiling to cover her sudden nervousness, she said, "Sir, if . . . if you are holding a pistol in your hand, I beg you will not use it. My word on it, I mean you no harm."

Wariness gave way to watchfulness. Suspicion became mere caution. Still, the slender, blond-haired man did not move. "And you are?" he asked quietly.

Choosing to ignore the fact that as the tenant, it was *she* who had the right to ask him questions, and not the other way around, Juliet said, "My name is Moseby. More importantly, I am a friend of long standing of both Alex and Tony Portman. Though at the moment I am rethinking the future of that relationship."

At last the gentleman relaxed. "Miss Juliet Moseby?"

"Why, yes. That is my name."

He smiled then. "It is, indeed, a pleasure to meet you, Miss Moseby. Though truth to tell, I feel I have known you for years."

"Forgive me, sir, but I do not understand."

"Of course you do not. My apologies, ma'am, but Alex has spoken of you so often that I feel I know you."

"Alex spoke to you about me?"

"Yes, ma'am. Though for some reason I had the

impression that you were still a schoolgirl in braids tied with ribbons."

This had to be the oddest conversation Juliet had ever had. A wounded man, wearing only a nightshirt and a few meters of bandage—a man she had never seen prior to this encounter—claimed to know her. Or to know of her.

"What did Alex tell you?"

"Nothing of which you would not approve, I assure you." He smiled again, albeit shyly. "When soldiers are far from home, with who knows what enemy waiting over the next hill, rifles at the ready, shared stories of home and friends are what keep a fellow sane."

"Ah," Juliet said, understanding at last, "you were in Alex's regiment."

"Captain Geofrey Lansdale, ma'am. At your service."

Politeness demanded that Juliet explain to the captain why she had felt free to burst in upon him—that the cottage had been lent to her for an indefinite period, and she was inspecting the rooms. Not surprisingly, the gentleman did not reciprocate by offering an explanation for his present occupation of the attic. Furthermore, if she read correctly his sudden fascination with a loose thread on his blanket, Geofrey Lansdale was embarrassed by the circumstances that had brought him to this place, so Juliet did not pursue the matter.

Instead, she begged the captain's pardon for intruding upon his privacy, then gathered her cloak around her in preparation to leave. "Before I go, Captain Lansdale, is there anything you need?"

"Yes, ma'am. A glass of water, if it would not be too much trouble. Some time during the night, I knocked over the jug Eisner left for me, and I have been praying this hour and more for something to soothe my parched throat."

He reached toward the bedside table to retrieve the

overturned jug, but the movement caused him to gasp and wrap his arms around his ribs. The way he eased himself back onto the cot, his eyes closed against the pain, left Juliet in no doubt that he was badly injured.

"Pray, do not exert yourself, Captain, for I can see that moving about is not in your best interest."

"You are very kind, Miss Moseby."

"Not at all," she said. "I wish there was some way I could relieve your present pain. Unfortunately, I have little experience with treating the sick and injured. I do not, however, believe that fetching you something to drink is beyond my capabilities."

Having committed herself to the errand, Juliet retrieved the thick crockery jug and slipped it out of sight beneath her cloak. "If I could do so, Captain, I would promise you your drink immediately. As it happens, I can make no such pledge. The world is wrapped in a fog this morning, so I dare not attempt to locate the well that supplies the cottage. For that reason, I must return to the manor house for the water, but I will return to you as quickly as possible."

At his sigh of relief, she smiled. "And if I can do so without raising suspicion, I might even commandeer a tankard of ale."

"Ale? I said you were kind, Miss Moseby. Now, of course, I see I did you an injustice, for you are surely an angel come down from heaven in answer to my prayers."

Juliet knew she was no angel, but as it turned out, she was also no mouse, which is what she needed to be to sneak into the still room off the Portman Park kitchen, then sneak out again without being seen by one of the scullery maids. Though she made it into the small, windowless room without detection, she soon realized that with no more experience in the kitchen than she had in the sick room, she was at a loss as to how to get the promised ale. It needed three hands to hold open the spout, tip the ale keg, and hold the tankard all at the same time. She was about to abandon the attempt when someone spoke just behind her, frightening her into a guilty gasp of surprise.

"Strong drink so early in the day, Juliet?"

"Alex!" she breathed, her hand over her heart to still its quickened pace. "Must you sneak up on me in that manner?"

"Not if you do not like it," he said. "Pray, in what manner would you prefer that I sneak up on you?"

The question being too foolish to dignify with an answer, Juliet ignored it. "You probably frightened at least a year off my life. However, this once I forgive you."

"Oh? And to what do I owe such magnanimity?"

Before she spoke, she looked toward the door, to assure herself that none of the servants had followed Alex into the still room. "I need you to help me fill this tankard. And before you search your brain for further clever comments regarding my drinking habits, allow me to inform you that the ale is not for me."

While his right eyebrow lifted in a way that said he questioned her veracity, he leaned carelessly against the doorjamb, with his arms folded across his chest, for all the world as if he had nothing better to do than to get to the bottom of her drinking problem. "If what you say is true, Juliet, and the ale is not for you, then you see me positively agog with curiosity to know for whom you have turned tavern maid."

Again she ignored his remark. "You will never guess what I discovered this morning, and of all places, in the attic at Auntie's Cottage."

Suddenly he straightened, all levity gone from his manner. "One can only guess, my dear Juliet. A bat, perhaps? I hear the creatures are frequent visitors to the upper stories."

"True, but that is your common, ordinary sort of bat. The particular species I encountered was unknown to me before today."

When Alex said nothing further, she continued. "I daresay the poor thing has known better days, for he appears to be suffering from a head wound, very tender ribs, and a dry throat."

"Common enough ailments among the bat population," Alex said. "However, until this moment I had not heard that the winged creatures liked ale."

"Ah," Juliet said, "then in this instance you must bow to my superior knowledge, for I have it on good authority that they like it prodigiously."

For several moments, Alex merely looked at her; then, as if it had been his plan all along, he told her he would meet her in the billiards room at eleven o'clock. "I know you have questions, and I will answer all of them at that time. For now, you will oblige me by returning to your bedchamber for your chocolate and toast, or whatever it is you take to break your fast. Meanwhile, I will see what I can do to relieve the suffering of that pesky bat."

By ten o'clock, the fog had lifted, leaving a gray sky filled with gauzy clouds, from which a timid sun peeped only intermittently. Juliet watched from her bedchamber window as a kittiwake glided on the cool late-summer air, his snow-white wings spread wide. Suddenly, as if eager to return to the sea, where food was plentiful, the lovely bird turned sharply and vanished into the clouds, until not even his distinctive black tail was visible.

Juliet envied the bird his freedom. How wonderful to soar, without a care in the world, then turn at will and go where your heart led you. She wished she might do the same. Unfortunately, Lady Feather's woman had scratched at Juliet's door only moments earlier, asking if she would come to her ladyship's suite before she went belowstairs.

Naturally, Juliet said she would join her ladyship directly; she owed this selfless woman far too much to ever deny her anything. Still, she hoped that whatever Lady Feather wished to see her about, it would not make her late for her meeting with Alex in the billiards room.

Juliet wanted to hear what Alex had to tell her about Captain Lansdale, and about the injury that obliged the gentleman to remain hidden in the cottage attic. But most of all, she just wanted to be with Alex . . . anywhere . . . at any time. After the Quick family left Portman Park, and she and Lady Feather removed to the cottage, there was no knowing when Juliet would see Alex again. Maybe never.

That happiness-robbing idea stayed with Juliet during most of the half hour she remained in Lady Feather's suite.

Clearly, the duel that had begun the evening before was far from over, for Lady Featherstone could speak of nothing else but "that woman" and her coming ways. That her ladyship was still in her dressing gown, with her iron-gray hair hidden beneath a sleep cap, and the rouge pots on her dressing table as yet untouched, was sufficient evidence that the dear soul had other, more important matters on her mind. The battle lines had been drawn, and she meant to take no prisoners.

"It is imperative, my dear Juliet, that we do all within our power to insure that Hermione Quick leaves Portman Park without either of her daughters becoming betrothed."

"Yes, ma'am."

Her ladyship, usually the least combatant of persons, was holding to this mutual dislike like a general holding to land dearly won in battle. So intent was she on planning her war strategy that little was required of Juliet save an occasional response.

"I just wished to be certain, Juliet, that we were in agreement about never leaving either of that vulgar creature's daughters alone with Anthony."

"With Tony? Of course not, ma'am."

"I know the boy is a scamp," she said, pausing only long enough to take a sip from her morning chocolate, "but I have no desire to see him forced into an unequal marriage simply because that woman claims he compromised one of her daughters."

"No, ma'am."

"And another thing . . ." Her ladyship continued in much the same vein for another ten minutes, with Juliet sitting quietly, lending only half an ear to what she was saying.

Her thoughts returned to last evening, and how handsome Alex had looked in his shirtsleeves, when she realized that the tall case clock at the end of the corridor had begun to strike the hour. With the eleventh chime, Juliet stood, asking Lady Feather's pardon for the interruption. "It is just that Al—er, Tony asked me to join him in the billiards room at eleven, and it is that time now."

From the look of pleasure that crossed Lady Feather's face, one might be forgiven for thinking she had just received a gift of great price. "In the billiards room, you say? What a marvelous idea, to be sure. If Anthony is with you, he cannot possibly be trapped by one of that woman's whey-faced chits."

"Very true," Juliet said, rising from her chair and hurrying to the door before Lady Feather thought of something more she wished to say. She had only just turned the knob when the dear lady remembered something.

"Oh, before you go, Juliet, do have a look among the things on that console table. A footman brought over the post from Stone House yesterday, and I believe he said there was a letter from London."

By "things" to be looked through, Lady Featherstone meant the peculiar detritus that was an unavoidable part of her, a result of her slightly scatterbrained persona. She was forever asking her maid or Juliet to search through the piles of clutter that covered most of the surfaces in her bedchamber, hoping to find some missing item or other. A lost glove. A misplaced fan. A priceless heirloom ring. There was no separating her ladyship from the ubiquitous clutter; Juliet had tried every imaginable organizational ploy, all to no avail.

Under ordinary circumstances, she would have groaned at a request to search through yet another accumulation of debris, but because she had been waiting none too patiently for word from the Bow Street runner she had hired to locate her father, Juliet dove into the mess.

"Have a care," Lady Feather cautioned when an open vial of sal volatile splattered to the floor, followed by a tin of face powder—thankfully empty.

Juliet muttered some sort of "fits-all" apology, for her concentration was on the stack of letters and cards of invitation someone had bound with a ribbon so none would get lost. "How much nicer," she said, quite certain the new mistress of Stone House had kept the dozen or so missives in hopes of annoying the dowager, "if the new Lady Featherstone had sent the post over as it arrived, instead of waiting until several day's worth had accumulated."

After removing the ribbon and tossing it atop the table, to become one with the other flotsam, Juliet flipped through the various missives until she found what she was looking for, a single sheet, folded and sealed, with her direction on the front. Since the letter bore a London postmark, she felt certain it was from Bow Street.

Now that word had arrived, Juliet found herself a mass of nerves, not at all certain she was ready to deal with what the detective might, or might not, have discovered. Deciding she would do much better to read the news in private, when she had time to absorb it without the interruption of well-meant questions, she folded the unopened missive into quarters. Then, with hands that were not quite steady, she slipped the letter inside the low neck of her dress, to rest safely between her shift and her bosom.

She would, of course, discuss the matter with Lady Feather at some later time, but not now. Only after she had had time for quiet reflection. For now, Alex was waiting for her, and she did not wish to be late. "I must run," she said.

After blowing a kiss to her ladyship, Juliet quit the bedchamber and hurried down the corridor. Since the billiards room was in the center of the ground floor, to the rear of the vestibule, she chose to use the more direct route, which was by way of the servants' stairs. Unfortunately, though she all but flew down the narrow wooden steps, she opened the door to the very masculine retreat to find it unoccupied.

Disappointment assailed her. Had Alex come and gone? Was she that late, that he could not wait for her? Did he even care that she had not been there at the appointed hour?

Discovering that the questions made her as despondent as the possible answers, Juliet walked over to one of a pair of floor-to-ceiling windows, where a leather-covered bench had been fitted into the embrasure. Perhaps it was Alex who was late. Hoping that was the case, she sat down to wait for him. When ten minutes passed and Alex had not put in an appearance, Juliet began to despair of his coming.

Angry with herself for allowing such an insignificant event to overset her usual calm, she called herself to task. "Such foolishness! It is not as if he is your

avowed swain and you are the declared object of his
regard."

The words acted as a warning not to make a specta-
cle of herself; unfortunately, they did nothing to ease
her disappointment. To take her mind off Alex and
his possible whereabouts, Juliet settled deeply into the
embrasure, with her back to the tall casement window
and her feet tucked beneath her. She retrieved the
London letter from its hiding place, and with
trembling fingers broke the businesslike gray wax seal.
Carefully she unfolded the single sheet, then slowly
began to read the brief message.

> *Bow Street Public Office*
> *London*

*Dear Miss Moseby,*

*A full report of my search for your father,
along with the agency's bill, is being readied
for mailing, and you should receive a packet
by post within a matter of days.*

*Meanwhile, there is something I felt you
should know immediately. Though my
search was not without hindrances (for full details of those unlooked-for difficulties, please
refer to my report) I did locate* Monsieur *Francois Du Monde.*

*Monsieur* Du Monde *(who no longer refers
to himself by that name) seemed to be genu-
inely surprised to hear of your existence,
though he made no attempt to deny the fact
that he might, indeed, be your father.*

*Though I endeavored (as you instructed) to
preserve your anonymity,* Monsieur *Du
Monde insisted upon being given your name
and direction.*

*The gentleman is (not to put too fine a point*

on it) a rather forceful individual, and one
not easily gainsaid. I regret to inform you that
I acceded to his request, and unless I am
much mistaken, the gentleman intends to make
himself known to you in the very near
future.

I trust this turn of events does not overset
you unduly, and that you will continue to
consider me . . .

Yr. Obt. Serv.
Wister Yarborough

# Chapter Six

*J*uliet read the letter through three times before she
allowed herself to trust that she understood the
rather unusual phrasing. There was one positive thing
at least: though her father had denied any previous
knowledge of her, he had not denied that she was
his daughter.

But what did the agent mean by "hindrances" to
his investigation? Renaming them "unlooked-for difficulties" obscured more than it revealed, leaving Juliet to suppose that the hindrances might as easily
refer to people as to circumstances.

And why did her father—"A rather forceful individual," Mr. Yarborough had called him—no longer refer
to himself by his French name? England was full of
French *emigre* families who had fled the terror. Surely
Francois Du Monde was not embarrassed to have es-
caped beheading by the sansculottes.

As to his having coerced her name and direction
from the Bow Street runner, Juliet was not at all certain how she felt about that. In all her imagined encounters with her unknown parent, it had always been
*she* who controlled the time and the place of their
initial meeting. *She* who maintained the element of
surprise.

Now, who could say when Du Monde might choose

to present himself on her doorstep? Or more precisely, on the doorstep at Stone House?

Not sure if the thought of his suddenly appearing, asking to see her, pleased or disturbed her, Juliet decided she must discuss the matter with Lady Feather. After all, her ladyship had graciously agreed to accompany Juliet to London to pursue any clues that might lead her to her father. Would she be equally gracious when presented with the information that some man whose entire background was a mystery to them might be knocking at their door at any minute? Seeking admittance into their home? Inclusion into their very lives?

Juliet was in the process of returning the letter to its hiding place between her shift and her bosom when she heard tapping on the casement window behind her. Turning quickly, she discovered Alex standing just on the other side of the embrasure, a rather boyish grin on his face and a horse's reins in his hands. The horse in question was Juliet's own roan mare, her pretty reddish-brown mane and tail plaited as if for some grand event, and with Juliet's own sidesaddle cinched on her back.

Much too excited to see Princess to give another thought to the contents of the letter, Juliet unlatched the window, stood on the leather-covered bench, and held her hands out to Alex, who helped her jump down to the ground. "Oh, Princess," she said, throwing her arms around the mare's neck and rubbing her face against the animal's velvety muzzle. "I am so happy to see you."

If Juliet's heart skipped a beat as well at sight of Alex, that could not be helped.

He was such a far cry from most of the young men she had met—fops whose major goal in life was to see whose shirt points reached the highest, or whose capacity for holding strong spirits exceeded those of his cronies. Alex Portman was neat in a military way, but the last thing he was concerned about was the cut of his clothes. As for strong spirits, she had never seen him exhibit the first signs of inebriation.

Alex was like no other man she had ever met. From the very core of his being there emanated vigor and glowing health, and Juliet doubted any female could see him and not feel the magnetism of his masculine energy. Even now, with his dark hair windblown and his top boots liberally splattered with mud, he was handsome enough to steal the breath right out of her body.

"Well," Alex said, observing her affection for the little mare, "if that is not just like you females. Fickle the lot of you."

Juliet knew from the teasing light in his eyes that his "grievance" with her entire sex was merely feigned. Still, she could not deny herself the pleasure of playing along. "Fickle? You would condemn all of womankind? Surely that is a bit harsh."

"Harsh, you say? Not a bit of it. Not when one considers the degree of my ill use."

Juliet forced her lips not to smile. "Your ill use?"

"Just so."

"Pray, explain this supposed ill usage, sir, for though I have searched my brain for transgressions committed, I find nothing for which I feel obliged to apologize."

He lifted his eyes heavenward, as if much put upon. "I go to all the trouble of taking myself over to Stone House, where, I might add, I was obliged to play the pretty to Lady Featherstone's successor for an interminable half hour, and what happens upon my return?"

He looked at her as if expecting her to answer the question. When she did not, he continued. "Do you throw your arms around my neck in abject gratitude for fetching your horse? You do not! You embrace the horse! And as if that were not enough, you rub your face against the animal's muzzle, all the while crooning your happiness at seeing her."

Moments ago, Juliet had experienced difficulty holding back her laughter. Now, suddenly, her problem was drawing sufficient air into her lungs.

"Have you any notion," Alex continued, obviously unaware of her breathlessness, "how long it has been since a young lady rubbed her face against mine? Or for that matter, how long it has been since anyone showed such unallayed happiness at seeing me again?"

Juliet could not think of a reasonable reply to that question, so she told herself that her wisest course of action would be to remain silent. Alex was teasing her, she had no doubt of that fact, yet there was a hint of something in his voice. Something that caused a momentary hitch in the pace of her heart.

Unable to stop herself, she said, "I am happy that you returned to us alive and whole, Alex. I prayed every night that you might be spared."

For some reason, probably because she had already revealed that much, it seemed the most natural thing in the world to reach up and placed her hand against Alex's cheek. The hard angle of his jaw against her palm sent a warmth all the way up her arm, and as if her thumb had a will of its own, it moved slowly across his firm, unsmiling lips.

The instant she touched him, his eyes lost that teasing light, and before she realized his intentions, he caught her hand and slipped it those few inches needed to position her palm where her thumb had been. At the feel of his lips against her palm, her nerve endings came alive, and the warmth that had been in her arm became a fire, a fire that threatened to engulf her.

All Juliet could think about was how much she wanted to feel Alex's lips pressed against hers. How much she longed to have his arms encircle her waist and pull her close against him. She had never wanted anything so much.

Not sure what to do with this unexpected fire, and embarrassed by her own wanton thoughts, she snatched her hand from his, giving voice to the first thing that came to mind. "Princess's muzzle is much softer than yours."

To her relief, Alex threw back his head and laughed. "That explains it then. Why young ladies prefer to nuzzle their mounts when there are willing gentlemen standing about."

Happy at the return of the previous light mood, and wishing to turn her back on the "willing gentleman" whose very presence made her act like some foolish schoolroom miss, Juliet took hold of Princess's bridle and blew softly into the mare's nostrils. The mare whickered a greeting in return. "Sweet girl," Juliet murmured.

When she felt in control of her senses once more, Juliet thanked Alex for fetching the mare. "It is a most welcome surprise, to be sure, but I do wonder why you brought her here."

"Is she not yours?"

"Yes, of course. But I—"

"Then she should be with you, here in the Park stables, where you need not forgo your morning ride. Especially," he added a bit too nonchalantly, "if we are to ride to the New Forest tomorrow."

"Oh?" she said, suspicious of his sudden interest in a speck of mud on his sleeve. "And are we to ride there?"

He nodded. "We are to make up a party."

"We?"

"Yes. You. Me. And both the Misses Quick."

"Both the young ladies? How, er, delightful."

"Isn't it just," he said, the dullness of his tone giving the lie to his words. "However, there are even more delights in store."

"More? I pray you, sir, remember that I am but a country lass, one unaccustomed to too much excitement. I doubt I shall prove equal to more than one delight per day."

He shook his head in emphatic denial of her statement. "In the past few years, I have learned to question many things, Juliet, but your fortitude is not one of them." Then, as if only just thinking of it, he said, "You would have made an excellent soldier, by the way. One I would have been proud to have in my regiment."

To say that Juliet was taken aback would be an understatement. Unfortunately, Alex had continued to speak, so she was obliged to tuck his rather unusual compliment into the farthestmost recesses of her heart, to bring out and ponder at some later date.

"Once our party reaches the New Forest," he said, "and a suitable stopping place is discovered, we are to partake of an alfresco breakfast. I hear they are all the rage among the *ton*."

Because she knew that Alex did not mingle with the *ton*, nor have the least desire to share in their often sybaritic lifestyle, Juliet assumed there was more to this unexpected outing than met the eye. "All the rage, eh? And you discovered that when?"

"Not an hour ago," he said, "when I was cornered— that is to say, when I chanced to meet Mrs. Quick waiting in the anteroom just off the vestibule."

Juliet could not suppress a chuckle. "So, the proverbial early bird lay in wait to catch the proverbial worm, did she?"

He put his hand over his heart, as if wounded to the core. "Not that I do not admire the way you get right to the heart of a matter, my dear Juliet, but do you think you might find an analogy in which I do not figure as a worm?"

This time she gave vent to the laughter bubbling inside her. "Why should you care? After all, *you* are not the worm the woman wishes to capture. It is Tony she desires to see become her son-in-law."

"While I," he said, his voice heavy with mock injury, "am a mere second son, and therefore of little interest to matchmaking mamas."

"Those are your words," she said, "and I beg you will not attempt to credit them to me. A second son you may be, but no one who knows you would be so shortsighted as to refer to you as a 'mere' anything."

"Madam," he said, making her an elegant bow, "I am unmanned by your kind words."

"As to that, sir, I should not be at all surprised if a far worse fate is in store for you on the morrow."

At his raised eyebrow, she said, "Mrs. Quick will probably wish to see you drawn and quartered when she discovers that her alfresco breakfast for three has grown to include a fourth." *Especially when that fourth is me.*

Not wanting to tell Alex that she had overheard the harridan suggesting to her daughters that Juliet might well be Tony's mistress, Juliet returned to the subject of the outing. "I collect you mean to have me come along to act as chaperon."

"As I said before, I do admire the way you go directly to the heart of a matter."

Understanding completely which of them was in need of chaperonage, Juliet asked if she should bring Morag as well. "She could remain beside you at all times, to make sure you are not forced into some secluded bower by one of the young ladies, and thereby compromised into an autumn wedding."

"An excellent idea," he said. "Though I risk appearing quite the coward, I am not too proud to hide behind a female's skirts. Especially if the alternative is to be obliged to choose between parson's mousetrap and my continued bachelor state."

"Too bad," Juliet said, "that our friend 'the bat' is not well enough to join in your little party. Another man might make all the difference."

"Shh," Alex said, all humor gone from his face.

Too late Juliet perceived the seriousness of the situation. "I am sorry. I had no idea—"

To her surprise, Alex caught her by the arm and began leading her, none too gently, in the direction of the stables, the mare's reins in his other hand. "Say nothing more," he warned, "until we are well beyond the hearing of any interested parties."

They were at the rear of the house, quite near the small square of land given over to the kitchen herb garden, but they had only to follow a footpath around the fragrant garden to the point where the path joined the carriageway. From there, the stables were in clear view. While they walked, Alex explained to Juliet the need for secrecy, not withholding from her any of the details about the thugs who had beaten Geofrey most cruelly, or about their employer, the sinister Mr. Worldly, who was adamant that Geofrey redeem his gambling vowels.

Juliet could not suppress a shudder. "Poor Captain Lansdale. And what a villain this Mr. Worldly must be. Might he actually kill the captain, do you think?"

"Tony seemed to think he might. According to my brother, Worldly's reputation for ruthlessness is well known in London. For that reason, I thought it best to get Geofrey to a safe place as quickly as possible."

Again Juliet shuddered. "So this is why you chose to impersonate Tony, so you could bring the captain here to the Park without anyone being the wiser?"

"It is."

Somehow, Juliet felt better knowing this entire episode was not some infantile prank. "It is not a bad plan, actually, for everyone knows that your brother comes to the Park on a regular basis. By presenting yourself as him, no one would be suspicious of your motives for leaving town."

"I was never keen on the idea of this playacting, but I bowed to expediency. Now that I have had time to consider the matter, it seems foolish in the extreme."

"You did what you had to do." After a moment's reflection, she said, "Are you quite certain that no one followed the two of you from town?"

"As certain as I can be. Now, of course, my primary objective is to remain vigilant, should any strangers suddenly appear in the neighborhood. As you will understand, I cannot afford to let just anyone know of Geofrey's presence at the cottage. The more people who know, the more likely they are, in all innocence, to say something in front of someone who would relay the information to those scoundrels in London."

When Alex looked directly at Juliet, she hurried to assure him that she would speak of the matter to no one. "You may rely upon me," she said, "for the very last thing I would want is to be the cause of bringing the monstrous Mr. Worldly to Portman Park."

# Chapter Seven

*T*hings do not always turn out as planned. Just as the ride to the New Forest for the alfresco breakfast was about to begin, it ended, and had to be postponed until the next day. No sooner had Nicholmore, the elderly butler, seen to the loading of the food and wine into the farm wagon, along with the table, chairs, linens, china, crystal, silver, and servants necessary to the success of the bucolic meal, than a post chaise came barreling down the carriageway, its team of job horses galloping at full speed, their heads bobbing and their manes flying in the wind.

The young postillion, in his regulation silk hat and his waist-length jacket, sat astride the lead horse, the reins in his gloved hands, but he was unable to stop the galloping pair before they reached the end of the carriageway. Their mad dash, plus their even more dramatic stop, startled the four saddled horses being held by two stable lads who waited beside the mounting block.

As a result of the equine onslaught, a large, rather showy black gelding, clearly believing himself challenged by the job horses, reared up on his back legs. Not surprisingly, the pretty little roan mare closest to the gelding's lethal front hooves threatened to pull free of the young groom's hold. Meanwhile, the other two saddle horses, their nostrils dilated by fear, did their best to break free so they might return to the safety of the stables.

Amid the bedlam of whinnying horses and shouting men, the door to the "yellow boy" flew open and Bob Ottway leapt to the ground. "You cowhanded idjet," the Welshman yelled at the postillion. "The man what give you that team to drive was an even bigger fool than you, and the two of you put together got more chockteeth in your head than brains. Now turn that team and walk 'em easylike to the gates and back so's they'll calm down, or I'll pull you off that leader and give you the pummeling of your life."

The postillion, apparently taking the threat seriously, turned the team and began walking them back up the carriageway.

"Here," the Welshman said to the stable lad who was trying valiantly to control the gelding, "give me the big fella, and you see to calming the little roan. And you," he said, to the other groom, "take those two back to the stable 'fore they hurt themselves. I see they be wearing ladies' saddles, and b'aint no lady with any sense going to ride either of them horses today. Not when they been frightened out of their minds."

No more inclined than the postillion to question the Welshman's authority, both grooms did as they were told, and within a matter of minutes peace reigned once again. At least as far as the equine population was concerned.

Unfortunately, the same could not be said for the humans who had materialized as if from thin air. At the sound of the ruckus, three scullery maids had come at a run from the kitchen, while from the front entrance Nicholmore and two of the footmen had hurried out to see what was amiss. Since Juliet and Beatrice Quick had been waiting just inside the vestibule for the arrival of the other two who were to make up the party, those two ladies gave in to curiosity as well and followed the servants to the carriageway.

Of the eight people who stood watching the drama unfold, only Juliet seemed to notice the tall, elegant gentleman who was picking himself up off the carriageway. Apparently he had been tossed through the open door when the postillion turned the post chaise, and as a result, his fashionable beaver hat lay several feet away, his neckcloth was askew, and smears of dirt decorated his beautifully cut blue coat and his once-pristine buff-colored pantaloons. Even at a distance, it was plain to see that his temper was at the boiling point.

Juliet had no idea who the sensible Welshman shouting the orders might be, but she had no difficulty recognizing the angry gentleman. It was Tony Portman.

"Damnation!" he said to no one in particular, "must a man be thrown to his death before anyone will have the decency to ask if he is injured?"

"Mr. Portman," Beatrice Quick said, confused to find him there, "how came you to be in that coach, when we were waiting for you in the vestibule?"

Since Tony was unacquainted with the young lady, and clearly had no idea what she was talking about, he merely stared at her, his anger growing more pronounced by the second. "Madam," he said, "are you deranged?"

Juliet knew this entire role-switching had been Tony's idea, and if the truth would have affected no one but him, she would have let him suffer the consequences of his thoughtless prank. There were, however, two other people involved—Alex and Captain Lansdale—and the captain's safety depended upon Tony's not letting the cat out of the bag.

Realizing that she must remind him that he was supposed to be Alex, she hurried toward him, her hands outstretched. "Alex! Dear, dear Alex. How wonderful to see you after all these years."

Tony, still angry over being ignominiously tossed head over tails after Ottway left the coach door open, ignored Juliet's outstretched hands. "Do not touch me," he said, "for I am all over dirt."

"Oh, Alex," she said, her voice overly loud to make her point, "as if I cared for a bit of dirt after *all this time*. Tell me, how long has it been since last we met? Seven years or more, I believe."

Tony gave her one long, questioning look, as if to assure himself that she was not foxed. Then, finally realizing that she had called him by his brother's name, he swallowed the animadversion he had been about to utter regarding her sanity. "Oh, yes. Yes, of course," he said, raising his voice so everyone gathered could hear. "Right you are. It is *I, Alex,* come home at last."

As an actor, he would not have toppled the great Garrick from his position as England's premier thespian, but at least he had not ruined everything. Taking Juliet's outstretched hands, he pulled her close for a hug. "Whew," he said directly into her ear, "I nearly forgot who I was supposed to be."

Juliet did not respond, as they were already being surrounded by Nicholmore and his minions, all of them desirous of greeting the returning war hero. Instead, she backed away so that the others might speak with him.

"Major Portman," the butler said, his face alight with pleasure, "how happy we all are to welcome you home. And I need not tell you how pleased Lord Bevin will be to have both his grandsons under his roof again."

Tony shook the butler's hand, as it was what Alex would have done. "Thank you, Nicholmore. It is good to be home."

He had no need to say more, for Alex was coming toward him, his arms open wide and his long strides eating up the distance between them. "Alex!" Alex said, sweeping his twin off his feet in a bear hug that was more punitive than affectionate. "You cannot know how happy I am to see you."

After enduring this completely bogus display of brotherly regard for several seconds, Tony said, "Put me down, you great oaf, before you crush my innards!"

The switch back to the brothers' true identities was delayed only by a brief reunion with his lordship in his bedchamber. For "Alex" to have delayed paying his respects to his grandfather would have been discourteous in the extreme. It was an emotional meeting, and it was as embarrassing to the real Alex as it was to Tony.

"My boy," the old gentleman said, embracing the grandson he believed he had not seen in two years, "you cannot know what a joy it is to see you again." After swiping at the tears that would not stop spilling from his eyes, Lord Bevin placed a hand on the shoulder of each twin, his pleasure a palpable thing. "My prayers have been answered, for I have both my grandsons with me at last."

After ten minutes of this emotion-charged reunion, Alex suggested that his brother might be in need of refreshing himself. "As you can see, sir, he has taken a spill and is in need of a washing."

"And a bracing cup of tea," his lordship suggested. "Have your man see to it straight away."

Not surprisingly, Tony pulled a face at the suggestion he would insult his innards with such an old woman's drink. Before he could ruin everything by giving voice to his wish for stronger drink, however, Alex gave him a shove toward the door.

"What say you, Grandfather," Alex asked over his shoulder, "do you feel up to meeting us one hour from now for a light nuncheon? The ladies and I were to have gone riding to the New Forest, but with, er, Alex's return, I feel sure they will understand if we postpone the outing until tomorrow."

"Of course, of course," his lordship replied, employing his handkerchief to wipe the remaining tears from his face. "Go now, and get our returning hero cleaned up. I will see you both presently. At which time, Alex, I hope to hear all that has transpired since last we met."

The brothers went to Alex's bedchamber, where Ottway was already removing clothing from a pair of leather valises. "Good day, Major," he said, a smile of greeting on his face.

"Ottway," Alex said, pumping his hand, "if I were any happier to see you, I vow I would fall on your neck and kiss you."

The imperturbable batman merely smiled, then turned to continue with his unpacking. "I took the liberty of bringing along a few of your own things," he said, placing a stack of freshly laundered linens on the bed beside a pair of straw-colored pantaloons— pantaloons the exact shade of the ones Alex wore.

"Good man," Alex said, looking at the sleeve of the russet-brown coat he wore. "I shall be most happy to resume wearing my own things, for I feel as though I might burst out of my brother's clothes at any moment."

"And I," Tony said, pointing to his mud-streaked pantaloons, "shall be most happy to rid myself of this dirt."

While Alex poured hot water from a pitcher into the bowl on the washstand, Ottway helped Tony remove his muddy outer garments. Then, when Tony began to wash his face and his hands, the servant turned to his own master. "If you will, Major, allow me to help you remove that coat. With both you gentlemen wearing straw-colored pantaloons, it needs only for you to give Mr. Portman the russet-brown coat you are wearing, and for you to don some other color. The pomona green, I'd suggest."

"Thank you, Ottway," Alex said, turning around to surrender the coat. "I knew I could depend upon you to straighten things out in the shortest time possible, and with the least amount of botheration."

Three quarters of an hour later, while the twins walked side by side down the wide stone stairs, Alex thanked his brother for arriving within the time he had agreed to. "Though I am happy for it, in all honesty, I did not expect you to make the break from you friends until the end of the week."

"As to that," Tony replied, "they deserted me. Bazemore stayed only a day, as he was obliged to attend his sister's wedding, and Claxton took to his bed straightaway with a bout of the ague."

"And the mill?"

Tony made a sound of disgust. "A dead bore. Nothing more than two farmhands swinging wildly at each other, with no science to speak of. And if that was not bad enough, the combatants—I will not call them pugilists—were so mismatched that the entire mill was finished in less time than it took me to jockey for a good spot to view the thing."

"A disappointment I am sure. But what of the buxom Cyprian with the unlikely name? Cerise, was it? Were her charms not sufficient to make up for the loss of your friends and the disappointing display of pugilism?"

This time Tony held up his hand as if to ward off further interrogation. "Please, I beg of you, Alex, do not speak to me again of females, for I have sworn off those of the weaker sex for good."

Alex smiled, knowing full well that his brother did

not mean a word of it. "Am I to understand that the red-haired beauty did not live up to your expectations?"

"As I said, do not let us discuss females. Especially those whose avarice is surpassed only by their total lack of brains, conversation, and amiability."

"So. You appreciate brains in a female, do you? If that is the case, then you should find at least one of our guests to your liking. Miss Beatrice Quick, though no match for her mother in, er, managerial skills, appears to have outdistanced both her parents in perspicacity."

"You don't mean the blonde chit who was with Juliet when I arrived?"

"Shh. You mean, when *I* arrived."

"Oh, yes. Right."

As they had reached the red drawing room, just to the right of the vestibule, they said nothing more; instead, they pasted smiles upon their faces before confronting the numerous guests in the house. When a footman opened the door, announcing both Mr. Anthony Portman and Major Alexander Portman, they were confronted by seven pairs of eyes, all of them trained on the two gentlemen who were very nearly identical.

Mrs. Quick gasped. "Oh, my. I had no idea they looked so much alike. How is a person to distinguish one from another?"

No one answered her question.

Lord Bevin, Juliet, Lady Featherstone, and all four members of the Quick family had been waiting with varying degrees of anticipation for the arrival of the twins, yet only one of those assembled knew which twin was which.

"Here they are at last," his lordship said. "Come in, lads. Come in."

That the old gentleman turned to Juliet, a question in his gaze, was not lost on Miss Beatrice Quick, and

Juliet felt that young lady's curious regard when she answered his lordship's unspoken request and approached the twins. "Alex," she said, walking directly to him and placing her arm on the sleeve of his pomona-green coat, "after you have greeted Lady Feather, pray allow me to make you known to Mrs. Quick and her daughters."

As if he had, indeed, just returned to Hampshire, Alex bowed over Lady Featherstone's hand, saying something very softly, for her ears only, something that caused natural color to bloom beneath the rouge on the older lady's cheeks. "You were ever a rogue," she said, attempting to hide the pleasure his whispered remark had given her, "and I see that life in the military has not yet made a gentleman of you."

"Did you think it might, ma'am?"

"One had hopes, my boy."

Alex merely smiled at her rejoinder, then turned and bowed to Mrs. Quick and her daughters. "Ladies," he said. "A pleasure."

Mrs. Quick gave him the shortest of civil replies, both the young ladies offered polite curtsies, and Mr. Claude Quick, looking a bit out of sorts as a result of last evening's intimate acquaintance with the brandy decanter, shook his hand.

The introductions finished, everyone found a place to sit; all except Alex, who leaned rather negligently against the mantel of the handsome marble fireplace. "Hours in a bouncing carriage," he said, employing the remark as both explanation and obfuscation.

"Not to mention," added their host, whose vigor appeared much improved by the knowledge that both his grandsons were safe and at home, "the bouncing you took on the carriageway."

"There is that," Alex replied, as if it had been he, and not Tony, who had been tossed into the dirt.

When his lordship commented upon his grandson's

much improved appearance, Alex said, "Indeed, sir, I *feel* better, now that I am my old self again."

The double entendre surprised a chuckle out of Juliet, and though she covered the sound by producing a sudden cough, Alex gave her a knowing look. Across the expanse of red-and-green Axminster carpet, their gazes met, and for a moment they shared a secret. They were in a room filled with people, yet that moment felt so private, so intimate, that they might have been alone, just Alex and Juliet.

Juliet felt cocooned in a delicious warmth. Had she been given the choice, she would have gazed forever into those compelling blue-gray eyes, and only through sheer determination was she able to break the contact, returning her attention to Miss Beatrice Quick, who sat beside her on the green brocade settee.

"It was the coat, was it not, Miss Moseby?"

"I beg your pardon?"

"You knew which twin was Mr. Alex Portman, because Mr. Tony Portman was wearing that russet brown when his brother arrived."

Though tempted to allow the pretty blonde to believe whatever she wished, Juliet appreciated the fact that at least one member of the Quick family had extended the hand of friendship. "For some reason," she said, being careful to keep that reason to herself, "I have always been able to tell which twin was Alex and which was Tony."

For everyone else in the room, the coat colors made all the difference, and it was not to be wondered at that Mrs. Hermione Quick gave little attention to the gentleman in pomona green. For the last two days, she had fawned over Alex, thinking he was Tony. Now, however, after only a few polite words to Alex, she gave her full attention to the heir. "Sir, my daughters were so disappointed that the alfresco breakfast had to be canceled."

For an instant, Tony looked bewildered, then Juliet stepped into the breach. "Did you not tell me, Tony, that the outing was merely postponed?"

He sent her a look that conveyed his gratitude for her intervention. "Exactly," he said. "Not cancelled, merely postponed. Which is a good thing, for now my brother can join the party."

From the disinterested look on Mrs. Quick's face, she cared little that a younger son was to be one of the party. Until, of course, Lord Bevin happened to ask Alex when he meant to visit his newly inherited property.

"Oh," Mrs. Quick said, a sudden spark of interest bringing a crocodilian smile to her lips. "You have property, Major?"

"Yes, ma'am. An estate only recently left to me by my mother's uncle."

" 'Tis a handsome place as I remember," his lordship said, "though it has been at least twenty years since I was last in Bridborne."

"Bridborne?" Mrs. Quick asked. "In Dorset?"

Waiting only for Alex's nod of assent, she said, "Our home is not twelve miles from the village of Bridborne. I take the girls there each month for the assemblies."

"Ah, the village boasts assembly rooms, does it? If that is the case, ma'am, then I feel certain we will meet upon occasion, for once I am established at the Grange, I mean to take part in whatever society the neighborhood has to offer."

"The Grange, you say! Surely you cannot mean *Osmond* Grange. Never tell me, Major, that you are Squire Osmond's heir."

At Alex's confirmation of the fact, the middle-aged lady's mouth fell open, and she all but threw herself upon his neck, so swift was she to offer him her congratulations upon his good fortune. Like a seeker who has just discovered *two* pots of gold at the end of the rainbow, the woman could not contain the happiness that rendered her positively giddy. "You must know, dear Major Portman, that the Grange contains a very handsome house, beautifully appointed with a number of very fine furnishings."

"I am pleased to hear—"

"And the estate," she added, clapping her hands together in her excitement. "Though not as imposing as Portman Park, of course, the Grange is none the less one of the most prosperous estates in the county. Why, I should not be surprised to discover that the rents alone bring in at least—"

"Papa!" Miss Beatrice Quick said, her pretty face grown pink with embarrassment at her mama's gaucherie, "do tell Lord Bevin that very amusing story you read in the *Times* about the Prince Regent's new phaeton."

The young lady's mama, clearly overjoyed at the discovery of two marriageable gentlemen of property—both of whom would be spending most of the following day in company with her daughters—took no offense at her offspring's interruption. In fact, she graciously allowed her husband to take the floor. "Yes, Claude, do tell his lordship about Prinny's latest folly, for I am persuaded he will be vastly entertained."

"Entertaining" was the absolute last word Juliet would have used to describe the story that followed. Unfortunately, while Mr. Claude Quick bored the occupants of the red drawing room with a retelling of an article that was as dull as it was never-ending, someone else was relating another story not four miles away, in the village of Buckler's Hard. In this instance, the narrator was none other than Cyrus Upjohn, the innkeeper at the Blue Lion, and the tale he imparted, Juliet would have found eminently interesting.

"Moved out of Stone House," the portly innkeeper informed the middle-aged gentleman who had only just arrived in a handsome, privately owned chaise. "Moved lock, stock, and barrel, as the saying goes. Both Lady Featherstone and the young miss as was used to be her ward."

"Her ward? Do you mean Miss Moseby?"

"Yes, sir. Come to live with her ladyship some thirteen or fourteen year ago, miss did, when she was no but a wee lass."

"I see."

When the gentleman raised his hand to brush into place a lock of black hair that was only slightly threaded with silver, the innkeeper was quick to notice that the cream-colored waistcoat beneath the stylishly cut maroon coat did not quite conceal a diamond cravat pin of impressive proportions. Ten minutes later, when Upjohn explained to his thin, tired-looking wife, who was both cook and maid of all work, why he chose to be so helpful to a foreigner—the sort of person he usually treated with ill-disguised disdain—he described to her how the late morning sun had been reflected off the diamond in that cravat pin.

"Practically blinded me, it did, and I says to myself, 'Cyrus, if you play your cards right, a generous vail should be acoming your way.' "

He held up a golden guinea so his helpmeet might admire it. "And this here canary bird proves I know how to get a bloke to part with his gelt. Even one of them blasted Frenchies."

His wife wiped her work-roughened hands on her apron, as if hopeful the coin might be passed on to her. To cover her disappointment when her husband ignored the expectant look in her eyes, she asked him what the gentleman wanted.

"First, he asks me if Lady Featherstone is in residence. Then, when I told him how her ladyship had moved out of Stone House, on account of the new baronet and his missus moving in, he asks do I know where she and Miss Moseby have gone."

A wolfish smile split the innkeeper's thick-jowled face. "That's when I played him like a fish. I gave him a look at the bait, saying how I might know something, then I hesitated, waiting until he reached into his pocket and brought out the guinea." Upjohn laughed aloud. "I tell you, it were all I could do to keep a straight face as I reeled that Frenchie in."

"What did you tell him?"

"The truth, of course. Everybody in the village knows that her ladyship is up at Portman Park, acting hostess for his lordship's guests."

His story told, the innkeeper bit the gold coin to assure himself that it was the genuine article, then slipped it into a small drawstring pouch he kept hidden beneath his leather smock. "He's in the common room now, writing a letter to her ladyship. When he's done with the thing, he says he'll pay half a crown to have one of the stable lads deliver it to the Park."

"Be he wanting some vittles?"

"Wants some tea, he said. Nothing else for now."

"You reckon he'll he be staying the night?"

"Mayhap, if he don't get a reply to his letter this afternoon."

"Is he gentry? The kind what'll pay for extra service?"

"From the looks of him, he's got gelt aplenty. He dresses fine, and he carries a handsome gold case for his visiting cards. I saw the card he means to send up to the Park with his letter. Not that I could read it. Got one of them outlandish names a decent Englishman can't get his tongue around."

As if suddenly realizing he might be overhead, Upjohn lowered his voice to a whisper. "As to the Frenchie being gentry, I take leave to doubt it. Gives me the creepies up my backbone, he does. It's something about his eyes. Cold, they be, and black as the bottom of night. For all his fancy trappings, he looks like he could hire on as hangman and do the job without so much as flinching. A real cold one is Monshewer Due Mondee."

# Chapter Eight

*M*onsieur Francois Du Monde's letter was delivered to the kitchen door of the manor house while Lord Bevin and his guests were still at table, partaking of a nuncheon to celebrate the homecoming of Major Alex Portman. With the butler at his post in the dining room, the cook took it upon herself to tell the stable lad from the Blue Lion to give her the letter and be on his way. "If her ladyship wishes to reply, she'll do so in her own good time."

Having dispatched the lad, who was inclined to argue that the gentleman at the inn was waiting for an answer, the cook sent a maid up to Lady Featherstone's bedchamber with instructions to place the missive in plain sight. Since no such place was immediately evident, not with so many personal items haphazardly strewn about, the maid put the folded sheets on the corner of the dressing table, which bore the least messy surface. Not surprisingly, the letter, like so many other things in her ladyship's private chamber, went unnoticed until the following morning.

Only when her ladyship's maid discovered the thick missive beneath the book of poems tossed there the evening before was *Monsieur* Du Monde's request read.

Thinking it must be an invitation of some sort, since

it bore only her name, with no direction, Lady Featherstone broke the inexpensive black wafer and unfolded the outer sheet. To her surprise, she found a second sheet inside the first, also secured with a wafer, and on the front of that inner sheet was written Juliet Moseby's name.

Her attention caught, she began to read the sheet addressed to her.

> Lady Featherstone,
>    I have it on good authority that the young
> lady who was once your ward, Miss Juliet
> Moseby, wishes to get in touch with me. I have
> come from London for no other reason than
> to put myself at her disposal. Will you be so
> good as to give the enclosed communication
> to Miss Moseby? I thank you in advance for
> your graciousness.
>
> Yr. Obt. Serv.<br>M. Francois Du Monde

Lady Featherstone, pleased that the writer had been gentleman enough not to correspond directly with an unmarried female, bid her maid deliver the letter right away to Juliet's bedchamber. Unfortunately, by that time Juliet was already on her way to the New Forest, having left ten minutes earlier, along with Alex and Tony Portman and both the Misses Quick.

Miss Celeste Quick, not a very comfortable horsewoman at the best of times, was nervous at the thought of riding for more than an hour on a horse that had sustained a fright only the day before. For that reason—and perhaps for another slightly more devious one—the young lady's mother had suggested that Mr. Tony Portman might be persuaded to take her younger daughter up in his curricle.

Tony had far too much town bronze to fall for that

ploy. Even so, he was unable to decline the honor without insulting his father's guests; thus he made a alternate suggestion—one that did not require him to spend several hours alone with a gently reared young lady whose mother was throwing her at his head.

"If I take the curricle," he said, "I shall be obliged to give most of my attention to the task of driving. I propose instead that we take Grandfather's landau. That way, John Coachman can mind the cattle, while I give myself the pleasure of conversing with as many of the young ladies as may wish to ride in the carriage."

Having outmaneuvered Mrs. Quick by supplying himself with a chaperon of sorts in the person of the coachman, Tony would not have been surprised if the next morning found both daughters dressed in riding habits and waiting to be tossed up into the saddle. In this he misjudged the young ladies, however, for both of them appeared in the vestibule in unpretentious carriage dresses and simple villager hats. Furthermore, if he was any judge of the matter, they were far more pleased at the prospect of traveling to the New Forest than they were at the prospect of traveling with a *premier parti*.

The day had dawned both mild and sunny, as beautiful a late-summer day as any Englishman could wish for, with a few puffy clouds floating across the blue sky and a light northeasterly wind. With such weather beckoning him outside, plus the added occasional cries of birds on the wing, Tony discovered that he was looking forward to the outing. The previous few days had turned out to be a real disappointment, and not just because the mill was uneventful, nor because the lovely Cerise had shown herself to be a brainless widgeon lacking the most basic of refinements.

If the truth be told, he had noticed several times during this past season in Town that activities he had once found amusing in the extreme had begun to pall. Friends whose company had never before failed to cheer him had begun to appear just a bit silly, and their concept of an enjoyable evening had become decidedly repetitious. In short, Tony was bored with Town life in general and with his cronies in particular.

He had actually enjoyed the previous evening, being in the bosom of his family. Perhaps that was why he had imbibed far less than his usual amount of brandy. Whatever the reason, the result had been that he had slept like a babe and awakened feeling more rested and with more vitality than he had felt in weeks.

After breaking his fast with a serving of basted eggs and kippers, both washed down with cups of hot, fragrant tea rather than his usual ale, he looked forward to a day spent in the fresh air. That his brother would be one of the company, along with Juliet, a friend of such long standing that he thought of her practically as a sister, only added to the promise of the day.

His chances for enjoyment doubled when he went belowstairs to find both Celeste and Beatrice Quick smiling shyly and ready to be helped into the landau. Some might think three a crowd, but as far as the heir to Portman Park was concerned, the presence of two ladies allowed him to relax, unafraid that he might tumble into some unforeseen situation wherein a lone young lady would be compromised.

Once the trio were settled in the landau, he called to Alex, who sat astride the black gelding Tony had purchased at Tattersall's auction only two months ago. "Ready to go?"

His brother said something to Juliet, who rode her roan mare, Princess, and at her nod the riders gave their horses the office and they took off at a gallop. The riders clearly did not want to find themselves eating the dust of the slower landau, and Tony did not blame them.

Because Portman Park was situated on land that blended seamlessly into the New Forest—the largest sweep of wild, uncultivated land in lowland England—within less than half an hour the landau was traveling in dappled shade, with thick stands of old-growth trees on either side of the narrow lane. The bushier trees—the elms, the hazels, and the junipers—grew amid the loftier trees, like younger brothers and sisters protected by their older siblings, the ash and the magnificent oaks.

Birds by the dozens set up a cacophony of whistles and calls as the humans invaded their territory, and while Miss Celeste Quick pointed out a peregrine falcon soaring overhead, hunting for his morning meal, a bushy-tailed fox dashed across the lane, catching Miss Beatrice Quick's attention. Without doubt, the young ladies were enjoying the drive, and though Tony was slow to realize that he was doing so, he began to see the forest through their eyes. The land was incomparable. Uplifting. One might even say spiritual, and he wondered why he had absented himself for so long.

Sycamores were everywhere, of course, as were the chestnuts, and when the coachman turned the landau onto a rutted path that lead to their ultimate destination, one particularly full-branched horse chestnut brushed against the sides of the coach. With a smile on her lips, Miss Beatrice Quick leaned forward in her seat, as if to impart a secret to Tony. "Sir," she said in what he decided was a whisper meant to be overheard, "pray advise your coachman not to drive too close to any more horse chestnuts."

"Oh?" Tony said, not loath to discover her purpose, "and why is that?"

"Because," she replied, winking at her younger sister, "Celeste can find conkers on the trees even this late in the season, and she possesses a lethal aim."

At this revelation, the young lady, who with only one

season to her credit had not become completely glossed over with sophistication, giggled like a schoolroom miss, then stuck her tongue out at her older sister. "You are jealous and you know it, Bea. Not," she added, speaking directly to Tony for the first time, "that I blame her. For you must know that Bea could not hit a barn if it stood a mere six feet in front of her."

Miss Beatrice laughed out loud, not the least bit offended by her sister's disclosure. Meanwhile Tony, who had already noticed that both girls were rather pretty, was interested to discover that when Miss Beatrice laughed, the animation took her countenance a step beyond conventional prettiness.

Of course, one had only to look at their mother to see that she had once been a very pretty woman, but Miss Beatrice possessed something more than her mother's looks. Actually, the sisters possessed an artless spontaneity that was as charming as it was unexpected—especially when one considered the mother's toadying behavior and the father's complete lack of character.

"When we arrive at our destination, Miss Celeste, I shall insist upon a demonstration of your lethal ability, for there is a shallow brook near by, where a very fertile horse chestnut grows. As boys, Alex and I were forever going there for our ammunition."

Miss Celeste readily agreed to the proposal. "And which of you is the better shot, sir? You or Major Portman?" Before he could answer, she grew pink-cheeked with embarrassment. "You *are* Mr. Portman, are you not?"

Tony laughed. "The answer to that, Miss Celeste, you must decide for yourself, for I never divulge that information."

The servants had chosen a perfect spot to set up the table for the alfresco breakfast. The beech trees

were so thick it was difficult to tell which of the min-
gled branches stemmed from which tree, and shafts of
sunlight were obliged to pierce their way through that
woodland cathedral to cast any light at all upon the
forest floor. Few plants survived in that dense shade,
but that circumstance was ideal for humans, as the
bog moss that flourished felt like a lush green carpet
beneath their feet.

The breakfast, which was eaten in mid-afternoon,
was topped off by peaches from one of the Portman
Park orchards, and it was during a comfortable lull in
the conversation that a doe, with her fawn close behind her, stepped out into the open. "Oh," Juliet whispered. "Look."

All eyes turned toward the deer. Unfortunately, the
skittish mother had caught the scent of humans and
fled, her spindly-legged fawn right behind her. One
minute they were there, the next they had completely
disappeared, swallowed up by the forest.

"How lovely," Miss Beatrice said. "I had not expected to see so much wildlife."

"Those are known as the king's deer," Tony said.
"You will see them everywhere, for this was once a
royal hunting preserve. The area has never been
fenced off, so the animals were allowed to roam and
populate at will, with only occasional culling by their
royal highnesses and their guests."

"All along the forest floor," Alex added, "one may
find the tracks of smaller animals, plus those of pigs,
donkeys, and the famous New Forest ponies."

"The very same horses," Tony added, "that bands
of smugglers once used to haul their tubs of brandy
and their packs of silks up from the Channel."

"Smugglers!" the sisters said at once.

Tony, perceiving their obvious fascination with the
subject, admonished the ladies to keep their voices
down, lest they be overheard by some weapon-

carrying miscreant. "What my brother did *not* tell you is that this stretch of the forest is now known as a smuggler's haven."

As he had expected, Miss Celeste's eyes grew round with awe. "Is it still, sir? A haven, I mean. Are 'the gentlemen' still active here?"

"As to that," he replied, "a wise man keeps his own counsel." When he raked his finger across his throat, making a gurgling sound meant to imitate the result of a murderous knife, everyone laughed save Miss Celeste.

"Behave yourself," Alex admonished his brother.

The young lady, her voice hushed, asked Juliet if what Mr. Portman said was true.

"Yes and no," Juliet replied. "Over that way," she said, pointing toward the east, "there is a deep ditch that runs for perhaps twenty miles. Its dense undergrowth once made it a popular route for contraband, for when in that ditch, the men who led the surefooted New Forest ponies were virtually hidden from sight."

"May we see the ditch?" Miss Celeste asked.

"Oh, no," Alex replied, his voiced filled with drama, " 'tis far too dangerous. Besides," he added, resuming his natural tone, "I doubt the boots you are wearing are stout enough to provide sufficient protection from the rough, wet terrain. I should hate to see you injured, Miss Celeste, especially before you demonstrate that lethal throwing ability your sister mentioned."

The meal finished, the entire party rose to follow Tony down to the shallow brook he had mentioned earlier, where that alleged fertile horse chestnut grew. Since Juliet had been there more than once, she hung back a little in order to ask Alex how Captain Lansdale fared that morning. "Tony mentioning possible injuries put me in mind of the captain, and I wondered if his condition had improved."

"Immeasurably," Alex replied. "So much so that he

is complaining of his continued confinement. Naturally, as a man of action he finds inactivity galling. I still believe, however, that he would be much wiser to remain out of sight."

"Speaking of being out of sight, I believe we have lost the others."

"Good," Alex said, looking around to assure himself that they were, indeed, alone, "for there is something I have been longing to do this hour and more."

Before Juliet could ask what that something was, Alex surprised her by slipping his arm around her waist and drawing her close against him, so close that she was obliged to place her hands on his broad chest to maintain some semblance of distance between them.

It was not to be wondered at that she experienced a wild fluttering in her midsection, but what surprised her was the difficulty she experienced in keeping her fingers still. Those willful members begged to be allowed to travel up the lapels of Alex's coat until they found themselves lost in his sun-streaked brown hair.

As if the thought granted permission for the act, Juliet felt those betraying fingers move ever so slightly toward Alex's neck. To make them obey her orders to remember who and what she was, she thrust her hands behind her back and laced the fingers together for safekeeping.

"Alex," she whispered, "what do you think you are doing?"

"I know what I am doing," he replied. "And unless I have forgotten how the thing is done, you should have at least an inkling of my intent."

She knew only what she *wanted* him to do, but choosing to pretend she did not, she said, "Release me this minute, before someone sees us."

"Not yet," he replied, "for holding you in my arms

was only the first thing I meant to do." Preferring action to words, he demonstrated the "second" thing by bending his head and claiming her lips.

Though Juliet had little experience receiving kisses, she was certain this was the sweetest one that had ever been given, and not just because his lips tasted of peaches. It was a soft kiss, for his lips, though firm, were gentle and undemanding.

"Umm," he whispered against her mouth, as if her lips, too, had been flavored by the sweet fruit. Then he kissed her again, this time moving his lips against hers, nipping, tasting, coaxing her to respond in a way that made her go limp with sensation.

He tightened his hold on her waist; then, as if to ensure their continued balance, he pressed his free hand against an ancient oak that was mere inches behind Juliet.

Unable to move, unable to breathe, she let him kiss her again and again, until she feared she would faint from the warm sensations that flooded her body, filling her with a longing she could not even name.

"Sweet, sweet Juliet," he murmured.

Though his words were like music to her senses, from somewhere Juliet found the strength to move her head back that half inch needed to break the kiss.

"Sir!" she said, her breath so ragged the single word was nearly inaudible, "How . . . how dare you?"

Alex pushed away from the tree, and though he loosened his hold on her, he did not remove his arm from around her waist. "Why so outraged," he whispered, his lips finding the pulse that beat wildly in her right temple. "Never tell me you mean to turn missish on me at this late date. Not after the dozens of times I kissed you in my youth."

Startled by this total fabrication, Juliet pushed against his chest, obliging him to release her completely. "You never kissed me, Alex! Not even once."

"Never?" he said, for all the world as if the information came as a total surprise to him.

"Never."

He laughed then, and the teasing light in his eyes was so appealing that Juliet wished he had resisted her push to separate them.

"I am certain I *wanted* to kiss you," he said, "for you were an uncommonly pretty chit."

"What a whisker! Alex Portman, you know I was nothing of the sort, for I was all bony elbows and skinned knees."

As if not hearing her words of protestation, he said, "Of course, you are pretty no longer."

"I am not?" she said, unable to hide the disappointment in her voice.

"No," he replied. "Now you are beautiful. The most beautiful woman I have ever known."

*The most beautiful woman I have ever known.*

All the way back to Portman Park, Juliet heard Alex's words, for they echoed again and again in her heart. He had said nothing more, for they had been joined by Tony and the sisters, and Alex had been obliged to pretend that they had paused in that spot to admire the clear, rich song of a skylark.

If Juliet had been asked, she would have sworn there was not a single bird in the entire forest, for the only song she could hear came from deep within her soul. Alex had held her close and kissed her, and it had been the most wonderful experience of her life.

Of course, she knew such kisses could never be repeated, for she dared not let down her guard. Loving him as she did, to indulge in an interlude that could lead nowhere would break her heart.

For now, though, she refused to think of anything but those tender moments they had shared beside the oak tree. The man she loved had kissed her, had even told her she was beautiful, and she wanted to bask in the warmth of those remembered kisses and those wonderful words for as long as possible. Later she would store the memories away, as she had stored the handkerchief he had given her years ago. But not now. Not yet.

"Just a little longer," she prayed, touching her fingertips to her lips, as if to aid her senses in their recall of those sweet kisses. "Please, God, do not let it end just yet."

Later that evening, when she should have been getting dressed for dinner, she tried once again to recall the feel of Alex's kiss. Unfortunately, she was startled from her reverie by Morag's question about some letter or other.

"What is it?" she asked.

"You've a letter, Miss Juliet. There on the dressing table. Lady Featherstone's maid brought it scarce ten minutes after you left this morning."

Only mildly interested, Juliet picked up the folded sheet and stared at her name written across the front, confused, because the handwriting was not Lady Feather's as she had expected. Though she did not recognize the handwriting, the bold script was clearly that of a man.

"There's a visiting card, too," Morag said. "It fell out of the letter, but I put it there on the table as well."

Setting the letter aside, Juliet lifted the small, cream-colored square of pasteboard and read the name engraved there. "Francois Du Monde," she said aloud, knowing that Morag, who could not read, was curious as to the letter-writer's identity.

The little pouter pigeon gasped, and her hand went to her plump bosom as if to assure herself that her heart had not stopped. "Ach, and 'tis too long since I heard that name. And too soon as well, I'm thinking."

Juliet knew full well Morag's opinion of the man who had broken Dora Moseby's heart. Morag thought him the devil incarnate, and she had never agreed with Juliet's desire to find her father.

Juliet's mother had loved Francois dearly. And yet he had left her waiting at the altar, with the vicar ready to read the marriage lines that would have saved her from years of heartbreak, not to mention from being branded no better than she should be. Dora had waited two full hours at the church, with Morag by her side, but Francois had not come as he had sworn he would, with a special license in hand.

Dora had returned to her home, with only a few weeks' grace before her condition became apparent. As she had feared, when her stepfather—himself a vicar of a small village parish—discovered that his wife's daughter was with child, he sent her away, with Morag to care for her and a small quarterly allowance to ease his conscience. Dora had been banished, and for the shame that had been visited upon her, Morag held Francois Du Monde totally responsible.

With hands that were none too steady, Juliet broke the black wafer, then unfolded the single sheet of paper.

*My dear Miss Moseby,*

*Some days ago I was approached by a Bow Street agent who gave me your name and a little information regarding your background. The agent said you had questions, and that you meant to come to London in search of answers.*

*I felt it would be more convenient, not to mention more private, if we met in some less populated location. I have come to Hampshire for no other purpose than to put myself at*

*your disposal. If you still wish to speak with
me, I will be waiting beside the footbridge
at the green at noonday. I shall be there both
today and tomorrow.*

*By the following day, if you have not come
to the green, I will assume that your questions are no longer pressing. At that time, I will
return to Town, with the understanding that
further contact between us is not your wish.*

*Awaiting your decision, I am . . .*
*Your Obt. Serv.*
*Francois Du Monde*

# Chapter Nine

*I*t was not to be wondered at that Juliet found the hours overlong between the time she read the letter and late morning the next day, when she set out for Buckler's Hard. She had meant to ride to the village, and had donned her new claret-colored habit with the jockey bonnet for three reasons. First, it was the most fashionable item she owned. Second, it was becoming to someone of her coloring. Third, whatever happened today, she wanted *Monsieur* Du Monde to leave Hampshire knowing that the child he had allowed to become an orphan had survived quite well without him, thank you very much!

At the last minute, Morag insisted upon accompanying Juliet to the village, obliging her to send Princess back to the stables in favor of the Park's pony cart. She did not, however, change the claret habit.

The cart, pulled by a soft-mouthed mare who was pleased to be out in the fresh air, was a lightweight conveyance with a basketlike seat woven of the local osiers. The seat was sufficient to hold two women comfortably, but what should have been a pleasant half-hour drive was rendered most unpleasant by the constant flow of advice offered by Morag.

"He's not to be trusted, Miss Juliet, so dinna forget it."

"No, I won't forget."

"And be mindful that you dinna tell him about the inheritance left you by dear Sir Titus. Like as not the blackguard's only come because he hopes to wheedle you out of your gelt."

Juliet did not bother reminding her loyal protector that only the two of them and Lady Feather knew of Sir Titus's generous bequest. Upon his death, the dear man had left Juliet ten thousand pounds. Not a great fortune, but more than enough to provide her with a comfortable life.

"Sir Titus meant that money for your dowry," Morag said, "and like as not he's turning in his grave this very minute, knowing you mean to risk it by exposing yourself to the devil himself."

Choosing to push from her mind the macabre image of corpses whirling in their graves, Juliet assured the Scotswoman that she would not discuss money with *Monsieur* Du Monde. "And should he fall on his knees at my feet and beg for nothing more than a crust of bread to assuage the pain of starvation, I promise to turn a deaf ear."

"Ach, now you've turned sulky, you have. And the good Lord knows there's no talking to you when you get that way."

Morag's having said, "There's no talking to you," did not mean for one moment that she had any intention of keeping her thoughts to herself. Even after Juliet had left the pony and cart at the blacksmith's and had turned to look up the high street toward the village green, Morag continued to impart words of wisdom.

"Yes, thank you, Morag. Now, if you please," Juliet said, pulling a paper from the pocket of her habit skirt, "here is a list of items I need from the draper's."

Though Morag looked as though she might argue that pins and thread could wait for another day, she

took the list and did as she was bid. "Fifteen minutes
I'll be," she said over her shoulder, "then its to the
green I'll be coming. I'll trust that devil for no longer
than that."

Alone at last, Juliet glanced at her reflection in the
glass of the saddler's window to assure herself that
her hat was straight and that no strands of hair had
come loose. Everything appeared to be in order, at
least outwardly. Inwardly, the situation was altogether
different, for her stomach had been tied in knots since
that first reading of Du Monde's letter. Reminding
herself that she had no reason to care what this man
thought of her, she turned from the saddler's window
and hurried toward the green.

A pretty stone footbridge arched over the shallow
brook beyond the green, and on the moist banks willow trees grew in abundance, their feathery leaves dip-
ping almost to the water. On the near bank was a
bench made of the same stone as the footbridge. The
bench had been placed there at least a century ago
for the benefit of those who wished to watch the many
birds who stopped to drink their fill and to search for
the bright blue dragonflies that liked to rest on the
mossy stones at the water's edge.

A man sat on the bench, his back to the green,
where a dozen Hampshire sheep grazed, their black
muzzles contrasting strongly with their fluffy white
wool. As Juliet drew near, the man must have sensed
her approach, for he rose and turned to face her. He
was not a tall man, not when one was accustomed to
looking at Alex and Tony. And he was quite slender,
though his posture was admirable, and he carried himself with such an air that a person might be forgiven
for thinking him a man of much sturdier build.

His was, without question, an imposing presence.
Though at that moment, Juliet could not say why she
believed it to be so.

"Good day," he said, lifting his hat and making her a bow elegant enough for a presentation at court.

The bright noonday light lent his black hair a bluish sheen, yet there was silver at his temples, an understandable fact since the man would soon be fifty years old. At close range, his complexion appeared fashionably pale, as if he seldom went out in the sun, though the skin around his eyes showed those fine lines one expected to see on a man of his age.

As for the remainder of his features, they lost importance the instant Juliet looked directly into his eyes. How could they not, when those brown orbs were clearly the originals from which her own had been copied. If she had harbored any doubts that this man was her father, one look into his eyes removed all uncertainty.

He must have felt the same, for when she offered him her hand, he took it in his and kissed her fingers. "Save for the eyes, *Mademoiselle,* you are your mother as she was twenty-five years ago."

"Twenty-seven," Juliet said, suspecting he had given the wrong number as a final test. "I turned twenty-six last Quarter Day."

*"Mais oui."* The words were uttered beneath his breath, as if he spoke to himself rather than to her. "That would be correct, for it was about this time of year that I met your mother."

"At Drury Lane, in London," Juliet added. "She was the guest of one of her school friends, who happened to be your cousin."

He nodded. Then, as if to ensure their privacy, he suggested they walk across the bridge. "Unless, of course, you would prefer to stay here. If that is so, I could offer you a cup of tea. There is a bakery just there," he said, pointing back toward the group of one- and two-story brick buildings that made up the village. "I saw tables inside when I passed the shop."

Juliet never went inside the bakery, because it was now operated by her childhood nemesis, Zeke Dobbs. He no longer taunted her, of course, but for understandable reasons, she preferred not to patronize his establishment. "I should prefer to walk, sir."

While they crossed to the other side of the brook, neither of them said a word. Juliet had a million questions, but now that the time had come to ask them, she had difficulty forming the words.

Du Monde, obviously feeling less conversational restraint, began by telling her that he had originally assumed she was Lady Featherstone's companion. "You will forgive me, my dear, but when the Bow Street agent told me of your existence, my first thought was that you searched for me because you were in need of money. Of course," he hurried to say, "the innkeeper of the Blue Lion unknowingly corrected that erroneous assumption when he informed me that you came to Hampshire as her ladyship's ward. And that you still resided with her."

Remembering her promise not to discuss money, Juliet said, "Sir Titus and Lady Feather were kindness itself to me." She said no more, merely let him make what he would of that disclosure. "My wish to find you, sir, had nothing to do with money. My sole purpose was to ask you why you left my mother to bear her disgrace alone."

"Ah, *Mademoiselle,* I see you do not bandy words."

"What would be the point, sir, when the answer to that single question determines whether or not I ask others, or merely turn and walk away."

Before he replied, he reached inside his coat and removed a folded paper that was yellowed with age. "I saved this," he said. "It is the special license I purchased so that Dora and I might be wed."

Only slightly mollified, she said, "If you meant to marry her, then why did you leave her waiting for you at the church?"

"The answer to that is simple. I was bound for the church when the hackney in which I traveled overturned." He pushed a lock of hair away from his forehead to reveal a thin scar perhaps two inches long. "I hit my head, and as a result of that injury, I lay unconscious for two days.

"When I finally came to myself, Dora was gone. She had left London. Though I begged my cousin to help me, all she would say was that Dora had returned to her home, and that she had left word that she wanted nothing more to do with me."

He paused for a moment. "We were both very young, but I loved her. The moment we met, I fell instantly and passionately in love. And I believe she shared my feelings."

As if he found the next remark difficult, he hesitated for several seconds. "I vow to you on my sacred honor, *Mademoiselle,* that had I known Dora was *enceinte,* I would have turned over heaven and earth to find her."

He reached inside his coat once again, only this time he removed a gold timepiece and depressed a small spring that opened the back of the case. A portrait, painted on a thin layer of ivory, had been fitted into the round opening. After looking at the miniature for several moments, he passed the timepiece to Juliet.

"In my youth," he said, "I dreamed of becoming a painter. Unfortunately, it was not to be, and all I have to show for my aspirations is this miniature. A portrait I did by memory, so I would never forget the only woman I ever loved."

Juliet took the timepiece and held it so the light shone on the miniature. The picture was of a young woman with light brown hair and blue eyes, and as Juliet gazed at the face she had not seen since she was a broken-hearted child of twelve, she felt tears pool in her eyes and slowly spill down her cheeks.

"Oh," she said. "She is so beautiful. And just as I remember her."

A quarter of a century had passed since Du Monde painted that portrait, and the idealistic young man he had been all those years ago was as dead as the subject herself, hardened by time and circumstances into the man he was now. The man he had become had grown immune to women's tears long ago, or so he believed.

To his amazement, he discovered that this young woman's silent weeping moved him more than he had thought possible. He had been unprepared for her distress upon seeing the portrait of her mother. Worse yet, he had been unprepared for the way her distress made him feel, as though he wished he could protect her from the pain. Resisting the urge to offer her his shoulder to cry on, he removed the clean linen handkerchief he carried and offered her that instead. "Allow me."

She accepted the handkerchief, and as she blotted away the tears, Du Monde wished he dared take the linen and do the job himself. Was this the way fathers felt? It must be. Otherwise, why would he have such a yearning to comfort this particular young lady? His child. His and Dora's Juliet.

"Since you already know that your mother and I met at Drury Lane," he said, "do you know as well the play that was being presented that night?"

Her watery smile told him that she did.

"It was *Romeo And Juliet*," he said. "Dora and I were not much older than that ill-fated pair on stage, and the moment I saw her, I understood how a man could be so consumed with love for a woman that he would rather die than live without her."

"And yet, you have lived without her all these years."

"True, *Mademoiselle*, but when I thought of her, I imagined her alive and well, with a husband and a house filled with children. And you must know that for the callow youth bewitched by love, a living *amour* is not nearly so romantic as one gone to her grave for love."

"No, I suppose not."

"Like me, *Mademoiselle,* you are a realist."

"Please," she said, "call me Juliet."

Du Monde watched her drive away in her pony cart, with the disapproving Scotswoman sitting beside her. He remembered the maid, for years ago she had tried to keep Dora from meeting him. Now, she protected Dora's child with even more fervent devotion.

He was relieved to know that Juliet had had such a loyal protector all these years, even though he was annoyed that Morag had interrupted his time with his daughter. The dour servant had stood close enough to them that the disapproval on her face was visible, and he might have been tempted to see if he could bribe her into going away for just a few more minutes, if Juliet had not risen from the stone bench and given him her hand in farewell.

"I shall wash the handkerchief," she said, "and return it to you." She looked at him then, and he saw a hint of wistfulness in her eyes—wistfulness rendered even more fragile by a shyness he was certain was not a usual part of her character. "Will . . . will you be here tomorrow, sir?"

He raised her fingers to his lips. "*Ma petite,* wild horses could not drag me away from this village."

She smiled, all shyness gone, and something twisted inside his chest where his heart had resided so many years ago. Looking down into that face that was the image of her mother's, he wondered just how different his life might have been if he had known Juliet was in the world, and that she was his child.

Not wanting to think about what might have been,

he released her hand and stepped back. *"Au revoir,"* he said. "Until tomorrow."

Du Monde waited until the pony cart was out of sight; then, thinking that tomorrow could not arrive fast enough to please him, he began to wonder how he might coax his daughter into remaining with him a bit longer. *His daughter.* The very words made him feel reborn. New again. Clean again.

Today's visit had been too brief to assimilate all the revelations; time was needed to allow them to be absorbed. Emotions had been roused, and Du Monde needed more time with Juliet so they might sort out their feelings together.

He had offered her tea today at the little bakery, but she had refused. What if he arranged for a proper tea tomorrow? Juliet Moseby was a gently reared young lady, and when presented with a fait accompli, good manners would oblige her to accept his offer of hospitality. Once committed, she would remain for at least an hour.

It would have to be outside, of course. For some reason, she hesitated when the bakery was mentioned, and until she chose to make it known that he was her father, he could not invite her into the inn. Not without a chaperon. The last thing he wished to do was compromise her reputation!

With his thoughts fixed on tomorrow's meeting, he had begun to retrace his steps to the Blue Lion when a movement in the doorway of the bakery caught his attention. The baker, a surly-looking bear of a man, stood just inside the shop, his thick, hairy arms crossed over his flour-spattered apron in an angry attitude, as if he had been kept waiting for someone. The fellow was probably no more than thirty, but the slackness of his full lips and the boredom reflected on his rather coarse, moon-shaped face made him appear older than his years.

"Ye that Frenchie what's staying at the Blue Lion? The one as is so free with his gelt?"

"I am French, yes. And for a short time, at least, I have a room at the inn." As for the question about his supposed generosity with money, he ignored that completely, though he suspected it was the man's primary reason for speaking to him.

"I been waiting for you," the baker said, his tone accusing.

"Have you now?" An excellent judge of character, Du Monde knew exactly what sort of man this was, for there were a thousand just like him in London. No, ten thousand. All of them malcontents who blamed everyone but themselves for their sorry situations in life.

The fellow uncrossed his arms and stepped over the threshold. "Could be I could do ye a favor. If the price were right."

No pigeon ripe for the plucking, Du Monde had learned a long time ago to beware of people offering to do him a favor. Such "kindnesses" had a way of costing dearly. "As it happens, *Monsieur,* I cannot think of anything that needs doing. Unless, of course, you are available to prepare a tea for tomorrow. One that could be served by the brook at the end of the green. Nothing fancy, mind you, but something that would please a lady?"

The lout made a scoffing noise. "Ye mean that whore's whelp? The one whose hand ye was slobbering over just now on the green?"

Instinctively, Du Monde reached for his sword stick, then remembered he had been so foolish as to leave the weapon in his room at the inn. *Bah! What ill luck. If ever a pig deserved to be stuck, it is this loutish baker.*

"That b'aint no lady," he continued. "Course them minor details don't always matter, not when a man's got an itch. Besides, the way I hear it, Frenchies b'aint all that particular." He laughed, as though he had made a joke, but the humor was short-lived. "She be comely enough, I guess, though not to my taste. Too skinny by half."

His fleshy lips parted in what might pass for a smile. "A bit past her prime, too. Of course," he added, pointing to Du Monde's head, "she be young enough to scratch the itch of a man's what's already getting snow on his roof."

Du Monde was not a man who let his temper rule his head; he would not have lasted long in his chosen profession if he had not learned early to show little and tell even less. Even so, he found it difficult to keep his voice from betraying his desire to see the man lying at his feet, with a goodly supply of his blood seeping onto the floor of the establishment.

Speaking slowly, so there was no mistaking his words, he said, "One must suppose, *Monsieur,* that you had a reason for introducing this very odd conversation. Pray, state it now, without further round-aboutation. What is it you want from me?"

"Ye want plain speaking, then plain speaking's what ye'll get. I saw you talking with her highness, and I saw how taken ye were with her."

"And?"

"And, if you've a mind to have her, I can make that happen. For a price."

Anger nearly choked him, but Du Monde managed to ask the lout just how he thought he could accomplish that feat.

"Nothing simpler." Too thickheaded to discern when true danger was near, the baker continued. "She rides in the lane every morning, and most times she's alone. It would be the work of a minute to spring out from behind the hedgerow, grab the horse's reins, and throw a sack over Miss Too-Good-For-The-Likes-Of-

Me Moseby. I could deliver her within the hour, to any place ye say."

"And your price for ruining a young woman life?"

As if he had been holding his breath in anticipation of that question, the lout exhaled loudly. "A hundred quid," he said. "And when ye've had your fill of her, old Zeke'll be glad to take her off your hands. No extra charge for that."

"Zeke? Is that your name? I should not wish to make a mistake about something so important."

"Zeke Dobbs," the baker said. "So? What do you think?"

"I think, *Monsieur* Dobbs, that you will be hearing from me soon. Very soon."

Half an hour later, the innkeeper at the Blue Lion scratched at the door of room number twenty-two.

"Enter," Du Monde called.

Beads of sweat gathered on the portly innkeeper's brow, attesting to the fact that climbing two flights of stairs was not one of his usual pastimes. He set the small tray on the bedside table and then, puffing like a bellows with a leak, he said, "Your brandy, sir. Will that be all?"

"Actually, Upjohn, I asked you to deliver the drink yourself because I believe you are just the man to see to a job that wants doing."

"A job, sir?"

"Close the door, *s'il vous plait*."

The man did as he was bid, and when Du Monde was reasonably certain of privacy, he reached beneath the cane-backed chair he occupied and retrieved a small leather pouch, tossing it to Upjohn, who caught it in midair.

If the jingle of the contents was not enough to convince the innkeeper of what was in the pouch, one squeeze told him all he needed to know.

"There are one hundred guineas there," Du Monde said.

Upjohn pressed the pouch against his heart, all but swooning at the thought of so much money. "Did you say one hundred?"

"I did. And there will be another hundred if and when I get what I want."

"An . . . another hundred." The afternoon sunlight filtering through the mullioned window glistened on the beads of sweet still spotting Upjohn's brow. Even so, he swallowed loudly, as if his mouth had gone completely dry. "You've only to name what you want, sir. Whatever it is, it's yours."

"No questions asked?"

"None, sir."

"Excellent, for I am in need of a pair of strong men who are not too particular about the way they earn their money."

"There are men hereabout, sir, who earn their bread by, er, shall we say, assisting in the transporting of foreign goods."

"Smugglers?"

"Transporters, sir."

"*Nom de Dieu,* I care not what they call themselves. I care only that they are prepared to fight if need be, and that they are not concerned about the amount of blood spilled—theirs or anyone else's." He paused, knowing to a nicety how his next words would be received. "I leave it to you to determine what their fee should be."

Never had words so pleased a man's heart, and Upjohn all but shouted for joy. Chancing to look directly at the Frenchman, however, he saw a coldness in the man's eyes that turned the sweat on his brow to ice. For just a moment, the innkeeper was tempted to return the pouch, for he had the feeling he was in the presence of Beelzebub himself. Luckily, the temptation passed.

"Do you know two such men?" the Frenchman asked.

"Yes, sir," Upjohn replied. "I know just the two you need."

# Chapter Ten

*O*n the return drive to Portman Park Morag was blessedly quiet, though the motive behind her reticence was not clear. Her silence might have been prompted by compassion, since she could not help but notice the puffiness left from Juliet's bout of tears. Or it might have been prompted by anger, for she had seen Juliet allow Du Monde to kiss her hand. Whatever the cause for the Scotswoman's behavior, Juliet was grateful, for it left her free to reflect upon all that had passed between her and the man who was her father.

*"Au revoir,"* he had said, "until tomorrow."

Tomorrow. Juliet prayed that by the time they met again she would have come to terms with her mixed feelings—feelings understandably influenced by having seen the miniature of her mother. As well, there were still a number of questions niggling at her brain.

The meeting had not gone as she had expected, for she had found herself drawn to Du Monde almost from the start. Not that she blamed herself for that. Not when he was everything a girl could want in a father. He was distinguished-looking, he was educated, and he was an artist—a talent they had in common. But more than that, he answered each of her questions with an impassioned honesty that was disarming.

Now that she considered the matter, however, she was not clear in her mind if he told her the truth, or merely what he thought she wanted to hear.

Where, she wondered, was that promised packet from the Bow Street agent? Perhaps the information in it could answer some of her questions regarding the man who was her father. If the packet had not arrived by the following day, Juliet decided, she would ride over to Stone House to see if the new Lady Featherstone was holding it hostage for some petty reason of her own.

Exhausted from so much emotional upheaval, Juliet was delighted when they reached the walled entrance to the Park and the pony cart passed beneath the stuccoed arch. The little mare was tired, and ready to be back in her stall, so Juliet did little more than hold the reins and let the animal travel at her own pace.

Her deep reverie was broken by the crackling sound of crushed stone shifting beneath the wheels of the cart, and she gave her attention to her surroundings just as they passed the thicket of blackthorn hedges that grew all around Auntie's Cottage. To her surprise, she saw Alex step outside and close the narrow front door. He had obviously been to look in on Captain Lansdale. What was not obvious was why he did not bother to disguise the fact that he had been inside the supposedly unoccupied cottage.

The answer came a moment later when Morag finally spoke, for she had assumed that the twin she saw was the heir. "There's Master Tony," she said. "Happen he's inspecting the cottage for his Lordship, just to see that everything is neat and tidy before Lady Featherstone has her things moved in. And high time he began taking an interest in estate matters, if you ask me, for it will all be his one of these days."

Recalling the need for secrecy regarding the captain, Juliet did not correct Morag's mistake, and when Alex waved at them, clearly meaning for Juliet to halt the mare, she was careful to call him by the wrong name. "Tony," she said rather loudly, "was there something you wanted?"

Never a slow top, Alex did not bat an eye at her greeting, but merely asked her if she had a few minutes to spare. At her nod, he glanced at the placid mare, then looked pointedly at Morag. "Can you drive that wild beast as far as the stables?"

"Ach, a wee bairn could drive that beastie."

"Excellent, for I wish to show Juliet something down at the weir." As if that statement might not be enough to explain his need to see her, he added, "I wager it is something she has not seen since she was a child."

A speculative look crossed Morag's face, and with a smile she took the reins from Juliet's hands. "Go on with you," she said, as if Juliet had been protesting that she meant to remain in the cart. "A nice walk is just what you need."

When Juliet would have reminded her that she had already had one nice walk that day, Morag said, "Help her down, Master Tony, there's a good lad."

The good lad, not a bit annoyed at being ordered about, stepped close to the cart, his arms outstretched. "Come along, Juliet, and do as Morag says."

Juliet reached out to give Alex her hands, but before she could guess his intention, he reached up and took her by the waist, lifting her down so easily she might have weighed no more than a child. Not that there was anything the least childlike in the way she responded to the feel of those big, capable hands—hands that held her long after her feet had touched the ground.

As for the look he gave her, that was pure adult male! The heat in those blue-gray orbs produced a corresponding heat inside Juliet that went all the way to her toes, a heat so intense that she marveled there was not a trail of smoke from his eyes to hers.

So locked were they in their own world that neither of them noticed the smile of satisfaction on Morag's face. "Come on, beastie," she said softly, "they dinna need us here. Besides, the sooner I get up to the house, the sooner her ladyship can give Mrs. Quick's nose the royal tweaking it deserves."

The cart was already on its way by the time Juliet stepped back, freeing herself from Alex's hypnotic hold. Feeling the need to say something, anything to cover the loud beating of her heart, she said, "Is this where you remark that I am as light as a feather?"

"I might," he said, putting his hand to his back as if in pain, "especially if the feather was attached to a wagonload of cannonballs."

When she pretended to be insulted, he laughed; then, as if suddenly remembering something, he grew serious, all signs of amusement gone. "Come," he said, offering her his arm, "I promised you a walk to the weir."

"So you did," she said, placing her hand on his arm.

The weir was to the south, at least a mile away, so they took a shortcut across the land that lay between the cottage and the pleached avenue. The wide expanse of grassy land was kept in check by several dozen sheep, and as Juliet and Alex continued down a natural and easy incline toward a tributary of the river, the only sound was the occasional bleating of a ewe, calling for her temporarily misplaced lamb.

The weir had been built across the narrow tributary some sixty or more years ago by the fifth Baron Bevin, Alex's great-grandfather, who hoped in vain to make this a prime fishing spot. Because the tributary itself was neither wide enough nor deep enough to attract the larger fish, the only creatures who seemed to congregate in the waters held back by the weir were minnows, crawfish, and water shrews.

Of course, the rickety wooden structure was now far too unstable for humans to cross, but Juliet had always loved this spot. A bower shaded by ancient beech trees, in the spring the entire area was clothed in wild flowers: blue forget-me-nots, yellow flag, and the delicate waterlily. To the young Juliet it had appeared a veritable Eden. Especially when her schoolboy neighbors would come down to swim—without the benefit of fig leaf—unaware that they were being watched by a lonely little girl who thought them only slightly less magnificent than gods.

The scent of the water spilling over the weir, plus the musky smell of decaying vegetation at the water's edge, had always made Juliet feel as if she could become a part of nature by merely breathing deeply of those earthy smells. Now, as she tried to recapture that feeling, the aroma that teased her senses was not woodsy; it was decidedly male. The fragrance of Alex's shaving soap, sweetened by the mist from the spilling water, filled her nostrils, making her long for him to take her in his arms and kiss her as he had done the day before when they were at the New Forest.

Because she knew that she should not be entertaining such thoughts, especially when she and Alex had no future together, she asked him why he had brought her here. "You said it was to view something I had not seen since I was a child." She looked all around her, discovering nothing all that unusual. "What is it?"

"Me," he said, "wearing a face of abject apology."

"Oh? Have you done something for which you need to apologize?"

He shrugged his broad shoulders. "You must be the judge of that. Obviously I have done something to offend you. And whatever it is, I am here to hand you my head on a platter, if necessary, so you will cease giving me the cut direct."

She must have looked as confused as she felt, for he said, "Did you or did you not sit at the dinner table last evening doing your best to pretend I was not in the room?"

"I did not."

"Play the innocent if you like, but in the interest of a friendship that has lasted for more than a dozen years, I would prefer that you be honest with me."

"On my oath, Alex, I have no idea what you mean."

He took her by the shoulders so she was obliged to look up at him. "Tell me truthfully, did I jeopardize our friendship yesterday when I kissed you?"

Her breath caught in her throat. How could he possibly think she was offended when she had all but swooned in his arms? Just the memory of his lips on hers, and the magic they wrought, made her knees grow weak. "Truly," she said, her voice not at all steady, "I was not offended by anything you did yesterday."

"Then why the coolness last evening? You barely spoke a word during dinner, and afterward you disappeared before the tea tray was brought in. Then, this morning, when I sent a maid to your room to ask if you would ride with me, she said you were not there." Clearly frustrated, he said, "Damnation, Juliet! Why did you disappear, if not to keep me at arm's length?"

Knowing she could not tell him how much his kisses had meant to her, she chose instead to tell him about the letter she had received from her father.

"Your father! I had no idea you even knew who he—" Alex stopped short, realizing what he had almost said. After silently calling himself a fool, he begged her pardon.

"You have no need to be on guard about what you say to me," she said. "We both know my background, so why pretend otherwise? Besides, it is as you mentioned earlier, our friendship goes back far enough that we can be honest with one another."

Honesty was a fine thing, but Alex saw no point in

carrying it to such extremes that it caused another pain or embarrassment. "What I meant to say was that I had no idea that you and your father communicated with one another."

"We had not done so until yesterday. He is here, in Hampshire, and in the letter I received from him, he asked if I would meet him in the village today. It was that meeting that occupied my mind last evening, to the exclusion of all else."

She appeared to wish to discuss the matter, so Alex suggested they moved away from the weir so there was no need to raise their voices above the sound of the falling water. When they came to a pollarded tree, he spread his handkerchief over the top of the trunk so she could sit without ruining her pretty habit. Once she was seated, she gave Alex what he was certain was an abbreviated version of the story, telling him about getting in touch with Bow Street, and about the resulting meeting with Francois Du Monde.

"There were so many things I wished to know," she said. "Things I have wondered about since I was a child."

This Alex could readily believe. Though he and Tony had been ten years old when their parents died—quite old enough to remember the way their mother and father had looked and acted—there were still things about them that he did not know. And he could have asked anyone, for his parents had been respectably married. Poor Juliet had not had that luxury. "And was *Monsieur* Du Monde forthcoming? Did his story satisfy your curiosity?"

"Yes and no. I was angry with him for so many years, as I am still, in those deepest recesses of my heart. Surely it is not to be wondered at that anger stored that deeply is not assuaged in one brief visit. And yet . . ."

"And yet?" he prompted, when she did not continue.

"And yet, I found I wanted to believe him. The

questions I might once have blurted out in anger, I was careful to phrase so they did not give offense. Even so, a part of me wonders if by being patient with my father I am being disloyal to my mother."

"On that score, at least, you may put your mind to rest. From all you have told me of your mother, she loved you very much. And though I never knew her, of one thing I am absolutely certain, that true love does not set limits. Quite the opposite, in fact, for it stretches boundaries. A caring mother would not wish you to burden your heart with mistrust, or with feelings of guilt, not on her account."

"I daresay you are right. My mother would have wanted me to be happy, no matter where I found that happiness."

"If you know that," he said, "does it not ease your uncertainty?"

Juliet sighed. "It should of course, but . . ."

"But what?"

"Nothing. I am probably being foolish. What I need is just a bit more time to sort through my feelings. Thankfully, Du Monde means to remain in the village for at least another day."

"You are meeting him again, then?"

She nodded, and for some reason, Alex wished she would allow him to accompany her. It would be presumptuous of him even to ask to be included in such a private meeting, especially when neither of the people involved were related to him. How could he intrude upon a possibly emotion-charged encounter? And yet, it was what he wished to do.

He had encouraged Juliet not to be suspicious, when suspicion had been his first reaction upon hearing of this Du Monde person. In truth, Alex had some real doubts. He did not like the idea of Juliet meeting this man alone; never mind that Du Monde claimed to be her father.

What proof had they that the man was not some

sort of charlatan? Being a biological parent did not miraculously wipe clean a slate of past wrongdoings. Just as being entrusted with children did not mean a person was worthy of that trust. Because *Monsieur* Du Monde was Juliet's father did not mean she was safe in his company. For all she knew, he might be a murderer a dozen times over.

Unfortunately, before Alex could think of a way to ask if he might come along tomorrow, a way that would not reveal his misgivings, or set up her back, he heard voices in the distance. Damnation! Someone was coming toward them. Could he never have more than a few stolen moments of privacy with her?

"Alex?" Tony called.

Swallowing a string of words unfit for a lady's ears, Alex answered his brother's call. "Over here, Tony."

Not wanting to squander the few seconds they had left, Alex reached out and closed his hands around Juliet's waist. He spared one of those precious seconds to just enjoy the feel of her luscious curves beneath his hands—the enticingly slim waist and the gently rounding hips. Unable to deny his feelings an instant longer, he lifted her off the pollarded tree, brought her close against him, then held her there, her feet not touching the ground.

"Beautiful Juliet," he whispered. Then, before she could breathe a word of protest, he covered her mouth with his.

Judging by the way she responded to his kiss, she had no thought of protesting. Far from it, for she moved her soft lips beneath his so sweetly that it drove him crazy with the desire to deepen the kiss, to elicit even more response. Even so, with his brother practically beside them, Alex was obliged to end the sweet embrace and set her down.

Her feet had only just touched the ground when Tony stepped around a growth of tall, thick lilac bushes. "Ah, there you two are," he said, apparently taking it for granted that his joining his brother and Juliet was a welcome event. "I did not see you right away. Heard you had come to the weir, though, so we thought we would join you."

The "we" turned out to be Tony and both the Misses Quick, and from the smiles on their faces, the young ladies had found their escort vastly amusing.

"Mr. Portman has been telling us, Major," Miss Beatrice Quick said, "about a few of the pranks you and he used to pull on unsuspecting schoolmates."

"Has he now?"

Ignoring his brother's unreceptive tone, Tony said, "My favorite was what we used to call the 'dropped pencil' trick." He looked at Alex. "Do you remember that one?"

"Actually," Alex replied, "I am doing my best to forget some of the idiotic stunts we pulled. And I cannot think these young ladies would find our school-boy pranks in the least interesting."

"But we do," Miss Celeste insisted. "Bea and I had governesses all our lives, so we never got to participate in the joys of a real schoolroom."

"Joys?" Alex asked. "Ma'am, if you believe Eton was a joyous experience, then my brother has failed to mention a few pertinent facts. The older boys were often mean-spirited, the classrooms were cold, the food was terrible, and Tony and I gained firsthand knowledge of the headmaster's conviction that sparing the rod would, indeed, spoil the child."

"Oh," the young lady said, her eyes filled with sympathy, "did you receive canings?"

"Often, Miss Celeste. Embarrassingly often. And if I remember correctly, one of those canings came as a direct result of our enacting the aforementioned 'dropped pencil' prank."

"Let me tell it," Tony said.

Without waiting for permission, he began telling the story of the new mathematics instructor, a reed-thin young man who was disliked on sight by every boy at school. "The silly old spindle-shanks was full of his own importance, and so new to the school that he had not yet learned that there was more than one Portman. By our schoolboy logic, those two facts alone made the fellow ripe for the tricking."

Noting that all three of the female members of his audience were having trouble controlling their laughter, Tony continued with his story, enjoying being the center of attention. "We had done this before," he said, "and the way we worked it was for one of us to hide beneath a desk at the far end of the classroom—"

"That 'one' was usually me," Alex said, with somewhat less enthusiasm for the retelling of the story.

Tony ignored his brother's interruption. "On that day, my brother hid beneath the distant desk, while I stood beside a desk located rather near the instructor's. There were at least two dozen students between me and Alex, all of them seated and waiting expectantly for the jest to begin."

"No," Miss Beatrice said, easily guessing the nature of the trick, "you did not, you naughty, naughty boys."

Tony chuckled, apparently pleased to share a laugh with a lady of her astuteness. "We did, Miss Bea, and it was marvelous."

"You did what?" Miss Celeste cried. "Hush, Bea, for I want to hear it all."

Not loath to comply with her wishes, Tony continued. "Just before old Spindle-shanks called the class to order, I let my pencil fall to the floor, then I said rather loudly, 'Oh, I have dropped my pencil.' Whereupon, I dove beneath the desk, making certain I could no longer be seen."

"Scarcely less than two seconds later," Alex said, taking up the story, "I popped up at the rear of the room, pencil in hand, and said, 'Here it is.' "

The ladies were already laughing at the absurd vision this tale conjured up, but Tony was not yet finished. "The best part is," he said, "that upon seeing Alex at the far side of the room, old Spindle-shanks shrieked, then his eyes rolled back in his head and he fainted dead away!"

"Oh," Miss Beatrice said, holding her arms against her aching sides, "please, say no more."

"Believe me," Alex informed her dryly, "there is nothing more to say."

"Except," his brother added, "that for a few hours we were the heroes of the school."

"Unfortunately," Alex said, putting an end to the story once and for all, "fame is fleeting. We were heroes for a matter of hours, but for an entire week following the incident, we were unable to sit down without the aid of a pillow beneath us."

Far from eliciting sympathy, this last piece of information caused all three ladies to laugh anew.

Because the entire company was in such good spirits, it was some time before they left the weir and made their way back up to the house, with Tony giving his arm to Bea and Celeste to assist them up the slight rise. Once again, Alex gave his arm to Juliet, with the two of them bringing up the rear.

Just before they reached the pleached avenue, Alex stopped, obliging Juliet to do likewise. He had been thinking about her going to the village the next day, and he had decided that he would insist upon accompanying her.

"Before we go inside," he said, "there is something I wish to ask you. Something important. Very important, actually. I wanted to ask you earlier, but I had trouble forming the question so you would not refuse me out of hand. Then we were interrupted before I got the opportunity to—"

"Come along, you two," Tony called. "Unless I am mistaken, I heard the first dinner gong sounding. And since I am quite famished, I do not wish to have dinner held up because my dawdling brother had insufficient time to dress."

Juliet heard little of what Tony said, for Alex's words were reverberating inside her head. He had wanted to ask her something very important. A question he was afraid she might refuse.

Her heart began to hammer inside her chest. Was she imagining things, or was that—could it be . . . No. It could not be! And yet, it sounded like the beginnings of a . . . No. And no again. Surely she was mistaken. Alex did not mean to imply that he was about to propose to her.

But what else could he mean?

He had said they were interrupted before he got the opportunity to ask his question, and at the time they were interrupted, he had been holding her against him and kissing her. Juliet knew where that delicious activity always led her thoughts. Had it led his there as well?

While these questions ran around and around in her brain, Alex took her elbow and together they walked briskly to catch up with the others. Just before they reached the house, he leaned down and whispered in her ear. "Be thinking 'Yes,' " he said.

# Chapter Eleven

*J*uliet made it to her bedchamber without any conscious knowledge of how she got there. She did not remember passing through the vestibule, and she had no recollection of climbing the stone staircase or walking down the corridor. She was conscious of nothing but Alex's parting words. "Be thinking 'Yes.'"

As if she could think of anything else!

Later, once the truth had come crashing in on her, she told herself that she should have thought through the entire conversation and held her elation in check until she received further clarification from Alex. As well, she should have remembered what she had known all along, that she and Alex had no chance at a future together.

Unfortunately, she did neither of the things she should have done. And the blame was entirely Morag's!

"Ach, Miss Juliet," she said the moment the door was closed, "you're a sly one, you are, to keep such a secret to yourself."

A secret? Still a bit bemused, Juliet could only stare at the Scotswoman, whose usually sober face was alight with a smile she could not contain.

"Dinna try to deny it," she said, "for I'd not believe a word. Not when I have the evidence of my very own eyes."

To Juliet's surprise, Morag was obliged to lift the hem of her white apron to wipe the tears that sprang to her eyes. "I'm that happy for you, Miss Juliet, and that's a fact, for I could see for myself that he has a real *tendre* for you."

The words were music to her ears. "You . . . you saw it?"

"Ach! Have I not got eyes in my head? How could a body not see it, the way he looked at you when he lifted you down from the pony cart." She actually giggled. "And making up that whisker about showing you something at the weir."

She helped Juliet remove her riding boots, then turned her around and began unfastening the habit so she could step out of it. Once that was accomplished, she gave her a gentle shove toward the washstand so she could wash her face and hands. While Juliet was lathering her hands, the Scotswoman sighed. " 'Tis all so romantic. As I told her ladyship—"

"You told Lady Feather?"

"Aye."

"I wish you had not."

"Dinna be silly, lass, for her ladyship was that pleased with the news. 'Depend upon it,' she said to me, 'the dear boy means to make Juliet a declaration down by the weir.' "

When Morag looked at her, her eyes filled with happy expectation, as if merely waiting for confirmation of Lady Feather's prophesy, Juliet spoke quietly. "He did not make me an offer."

Unaccountably embarrassed by the admission, in view of all this jubilant reaction, she applied the soapy lather to her face, as if she might hide behind the bubbles. After rinsing the soap from her face and neck, then drying with the towel Morag held out to her, she realized the servant's face had fallen with the news that there had been no proposal.

"As it happened," she said, "he did not have time

to make me an offer. Our time alone was interrupted by his brother and the Quick sisters.''

"Ach, them two," Morag said, fetching the blue moire silk dinner dress she had felt appropriate for the evening to come. "And won't that she-devil as is their mother be shocked to discover that her machinations were all for naught. That it'll be you as will be the new mistress of Portman Park.''

Morag had just tossed the moire over Juliet's head, so she had to work her way through the fullness of the silk skirt and then through the snug bodice before she could ask Morag what she was talking about. "I will never be mistress here at the Park.''

"Of course you will, lass." Morag busied herself with the buttons at the back of the dress. "His lordship, God bless him, cannot live forever, and as Master Tony's wife, you will be—"

"Tony!"

"Well, of course. Who else were we talking about?''

Juliet whirled around to look at the Scotswoman, feeling for all the world as if she had somehow wandered into Bedlam and was speaking with one of the deranged inmates. She was about to ask whatever made Morag think Tony had a *tendre* for her, when she remembered seeing Alex come out of the cottage and thinking it best to call him by his brother's name. "Oh, no," she groaned. "Please say you did not tell Lady Feather it was Tony who took me to the weir.''

"And who should I be telling her took you there, if not Master Tony?''

Juliet bit her lip to keep from screaming. "That was not Tony who helped me down from the pony cart. It was Alex.''

"Master Alex? But you said . . ." She closed her eyes, as if not wanting to look at Juliet. "You said it was Master Tony, and you always know which twin is which. If I had known, I never would have . . .''

From the sudden red that crept into the woman's

face, Juliet suspected she did not want to hear whatever it was that Morag could not bring herself to say.

"Out with it, Morag. What else have you done?"

"As to that, it's no what I've done. It's what her ladyship means to do."

Juliet groaned again.

"Dinna worry, lass. Perhaps you can catch her before she tells him."

"*Him?* Him who?"

"Lord Bevin. Lady Featherstone wrote a note asking his lordship to meet her in his bookroom before dinner, as she had something important to tell him. I delivered the note to his lordship's man an hour ago."

Wanting to scream, yet afraid to waste the minute such action would require, Juliet fled the room, her destination Lady Feather's bedchamber.

"Wait, Miss Juliet! You've forgotten your shoes."

Shoes were the last thing on Juliet's mind, for to her horror, she found her ladyship's bedchamber empty. Thinking only to catch her before she spoke to Lord Bevin, she lifted her skirts and positively ran down the stairs. Ignoring the startled footman who waited in the vestibule, she hurried down the corridor to the left, not stopping until she reached the bookroom. The door was slightly ajar, and to Juliet's dismay, she heard two voices inside.

Hoping she had arrived in time, she remained silently by the door, to listen for just a moment. With the first overheard sentence, however, she knew she was too late. She braced herself for the embarrassment of what they *might* be saying, only to be totally humiliated by the *actual* words.

"But I do not understand," Lady Feather said, confusion in her voice. "I thought you liked Juliet."

"I do," Lord Bevin replied. "I have always been fond of her. But not for an instant have I ever entertained the thought of her becoming mistress of Portman Park. You must know, Guinevere, that she simply will not do. Anthony must look higher for the next Lady Bevin."

Though mortified, Juliet comforted herself with the knowledge that she had no desire to become the heir's wife. It was Alex she loved. Alex whom she had always loved.

"You and I have been friends for more than forty years, Guinevere, and I have no wish to offend you. But the simple truth is that I expect both my grandsons to look higher than Juliet Moseby. To that end, I have made my wishes quite plain to them, and they know exactly the sort of wife they are to choose."

"But what if Anthony has already proposed to her? Surely you would not—"

"He will not have proposed, I can promise you that. Not a proposal of *marriage* in any event. Not to someone's natural daughter."

Lady Featherstone gasped, and Juliet was obliged to bite back a sob. Not because of what his lordship had called her, but because of his thinly veiled innuendo that his grandson would offer her an indecent proposal.

She leaned her forehead against the door frame. "Please," she prayed, "do not let it be so."

With a painful clarity, she recalled Alex's exact words to her earlier. "I had trouble forming the question," he had said, "so that you would not refuse me out of hand."

Why would he fear a refusal? Unless, of course, he had wished to make her an indecent proposal?

For as long as she could remember, Juliet had told herself that Alex would never marry her. Even to hope that he would return her love had been an impossible dream. Still, she had dreamed it. And until Lord Bevin had spoken those terrible words, she had been able to maintain that shred of hope.

Now, of course, she saw that she had been deluding herself all along. Fooling herself into believing that the indisputable fact of her birth would not weigh with Alex. He was a Portman, and second in line to an old and respected title. She, on the other hand, was the illegitimate daughter of a Frenchman named Du Monde.

With her lips trembling and her legs shaking so badly they threatened to give way beneath her, Juliet backed away from the bookroom door. Using the servants' stairs so she might avoid meeting anyone coming down for dinner, she hurried to her bedchamber. Once inside, she shut the door and bid Morag help her out of her dress. "Then I wish you to take a message to the butler saying that I am indisposed and will not join the family for dinner."

"Miss Juliet! What in the world has happened to—"

"If you have any affection for me," she added, her voice husky with unshed tears, "you will remain belowstairs for an hour or so, so that I may have some privacy. I need to make an important decision, and I must be alone to think it through."

"I will do as you ask, lass, only—"

"Thank you. Now, please go."

Morag said no more, merely hung the blue moire gown in the chiffonnier, then let herself quietly out of the room. For a moment she considered going in search of Lady Featherstone, to tell her about Juliet's distress. She soon discarded that idea, however, and made her way down the servants' stairs to find the butler and deliver her message.

As it turned out, Lady Featherstone was also absent from the dinner table. Like Juliet, she sent word belowstairs that she was indisposed, and the next morning, after having passed a wretched night, she asked her woman to see if Juliet was awake yet. "If so, pray ask her to come to me at once, for there is something of importance we must discuss."

Within five minutes, Juliet was seated by the elderly lady's bedside, holding her hand. It was obvious Lady Feather had been crying, for the face beneath the pretty lace bed cap was strained, every age line showing. Though Juliet knew the reason for her friend's misery, she chose not to mention the conversation she had overheard outside Lord Bevin's bookroom, and as if by common consent, the ladies avoided the subject of any and all members of the Portman family.

"Lady Feather, do not distress yourself. All will be well, I promise you."

"My dear, you are such a comfort to me. Had you been born of my body, you could not have been dearer to my heart. I have always considered you the daughter I never had. And Titus felt the same."

"I know," Juliet whispered.

After swallowing the tight knot that formed in her throat, she pressed the dear lady's hand to her cheek. "You were both kindness itself to me, ma'am, and I do not think my broken heart would ever have mended had it not been for you and dear Sir Titus. Now, let us speak of that no more. Instead, tell me what I can do to relieve your present sadness."

Her ladyship dabbed at her nose with a dainty handkerchief. "You will think me a foolish old woman, and I beg you not to ask me any questions, but I wish to leave here as soon as may be."

There was no need for questions, because Juliet already knew why Lady Feather wished to leave. Since this was the same course of action Juliet had decided upon the night before, she was quick to agree. "It shall be as you wish, ma'am. But just so I am certain that I understand you, do you mean that you wish to remove to the cottage?"

"I do not!" Her ladyship's face showed animation for the first time since Juliet had entered the room. "I wish to leave this estate, hopefully never to return again. I realize that you are to meet that Frenchman again today in the village, but once that business is finished, I should like to leave immediately for Tunbridge Wells or for Bath. Whichever place suits you best."

"Bath, I think, ma'am. If we do not find the company to our liking there, then we can try Tunbridge Wells at some later date. Shall I see to the hiring of a carriage while I am in the village?"

"An excellent scheme, my dear. Meanwhile, I will instruct my woman to begin packing."

The immediate decisions made, Juliet returned to her bedchamber to dress for her ride to the village. If all went well during today's meeting, she would tell her father of her plans to leave Buckler's Hard for Bath. If they did not go well, she would keep her own counsel and let him return to London none the wiser. The newfound relationship, such as it was, would then die of its own accord, and her life would go on much as she had envisioned it a week ago, with her and Lady Feather making a home together.

"You rode here alone?" Francois Du Monde asked, genuine concern in his voice. "I wish you will not do so again, Juliet, for there is real danger on the roads. With more knaves about than you might imagine."

Juliet shifted her position on the stone bench, then reached for her cup, lifting it to her lips and taking sips of the hot, pungent tea. Her father had ordered a tray loaded with pretty little sandwiches and dainty seed cakes to be served here by the brook. Unfortunately, a little tea was all she could manage, for she had no appetite. Not after the appalling news she had heard about Zekiel Dobbs.

"I collect, sir, that you are thinking about what happened last night, with the vicious attack upon the baker."

"So, you know. I had hoped you would not hear of it."

"In a village this size?" She smiled over her cup. "It is obvious that you have spent most of your life in heavily populated cities."

He returned her smile. "London," he said, "and before that in Paris. I prefer cities. In them, one may remain anonymous."

"In the country, sir, anonymity is but a word. Anything that happens in a small village is food for the gossips. No matter how insignificant the incident, it spreads with the rapidity of a forest fire to become the topic of conversation for days, even weeks."

Juliet took another sip of her tea, then set the cup back on the tray. "Forgive me for not partaking of these lovely refreshments, sir, but I cannot rid my mind of last night's violence. It was all they could talk about at the blacksmith's shop where I left my mare, and I now have such a vivid picture in my mind that I find it difficult to swallow."

Du Monde had reached for a sandwich, but now he drew back his hand. "Of course," he said. "One cannot expect to retain an appetite after hearing such distressing news."

She looked toward the brook for a time, as if allowing the gentle swaying of the feathery willow leaves to calm her senses. "Can you imagine," she said, returning her attention to him, "the sort of monster who would commit such a heinous act?"

"Mine is not an imaginative nature."

His answer, though evasive, must have satisfied her, for she continued to speak of last night's beating of the baker. "Of course, it is terrible that anyone, even Zeke, should be set upon. Especially when the injuries received are so grievous that the victim cannot leave his bed. You must know, however, that he is a bully of long standing. It would not surprise me to discover that his enemies are legion."

"You knew the man, then?"

"From my childhood. And as I said, he was ever a bully."

Du Monde had always been quick to hear the words people did not say, and from the constraint in his daughter's voice, he could guess that the baker had tried his bullying tactics on her at some time. *Damn his eyes!*

"So that is why you refused my offer of tea in the bakery yesterday? It was not my presence you objected to, it was the baker's."

She looked down at her folded hands, as if embarrassed by the question. "Whenever possible, I avoid being near Zeke."

The very idea that his daughter would be obliged to avoid a bully year after year made Du Monde's blood heat to the boiling point. If he had not already seen to it that the baker was rendered immobile, so that he could not carry out his proposed plan to kidnap Juliet, Du Monde would have been tempted to seek his own brand of justice for sins the despicable fellow had committed in the past.

Without realizing he spoke aloud, he said, "What manner of man believes it permissible to bully a little girl?"

"What manner, indeed," she replied. "But let us speak no more of Zekiel Dobbs, for after tomorrow, I need never look upon his face again."

"Oh? And why is that?"

Du Monde did not think the question a difficult one, but she seemed to need to weigh her answer. "Because," she said at last, "Lady Feather and I have decided to leave Buckler's Hard for good."

Surprised to hear of this move, he studied her face so he might read the reply to his next question. "This is very sudden. Has your leaving anything to do with my coming here?"

She shook her head, and to his relief, her face told him that she spoke the truth. "Our stay at Portman

Park was never meant to be permanent. It has always been our plan—Lady Feather's and mine—that at some future date we would purchase a home of our own, preferably in some felicitous spot where we might mingle freely with a wider range of society."

"At some future date? But you mentioned tomorrow. Has something occurred to force the future into the present?"

The pink that colored her cheeks showed him that he had stumbled upon the truth. "I would rather not discuss this matter further, sir, if you do not mind."

He minded very much, but he was an excellent card player, and he knew when to bid and when to pass. Now was not the time to force the issue. Perhaps later, when he knew her better, when she knew him better, she might come to trust him. For now, all he could do was offer his assistance in the matter of their travel. "Has Lady Featherstone a traveling chaise?"

"No, but one of the tasks I was to execute while in the village was to see to the hiring of a carriage and a coachman or postillion."

"A coachman by all means. And a pair of outriders," he added, "for your protection."

Before she could reply to his suggestion, he said, "If you will allow it, I should like to see to the outriders myself. In fact, I wish you would permit me to put my carriage at your disposal, for the vehicle is new and well sprung, and you would find it much more comfortable than a hired conveyance."

"That is most generous of you, but—"

"Please. My coachman can take you and Lady Featherstone to whatever destination you wish, then return to me in London."

"But we cannot take your carriage, sir. What of your own needs?"

He shrugged. "I shall do quite well with a yellow boy from the inn."

When she looked as if she might protest, he brought

the subject to a close. "Please, Juliet, allow me to do this. It would mean so much to me."

After several moments' thought, she nodded her consent. "As you wish, sir. And thank you."

She bestowed upon him a smile that he would not have traded for a year's worth of winnings at his gambling establishment, and when his heart had quieted, he lifted her hand to his lips. "It is I who should thank you."

She rose to take her leave of him then, but he insisted upon escorting her to the blacksmith's shop, where he gave one of the smith's sons a half crown to ride along with Juliet back to Portman Park. She protested, of course, but the youth had already caught the coin in midair and was hurrying to saddle his horse.

"Please," Du Monde said. "Do it for me."

She said no more, merely put her booted foot in his cupped hands and allowed him to toss her into the saddle. Once she was seated atop her little roan mare, he handed her the reins. "Do you mean to make an early start tomorrow?"

She chuckled. "I should like to do so, but Lady Feather is a notorious slugabed."

"Then I will not send the carriage around to Portman Park before midmorning."

"Midmorning would be perfect, sir." She held her hand down to him and he took it in both of his. "Until we meet again," she said.

"Until then, daughter."

Juliet spent the remainder of the day in her bedchamber, writing letters of farewell to the vicar's wife and to two other neighbors she considered her friends. Some time around four, Alex sent up a note asking her to join him for a walk in the garden. She refused, using as her excuse a headache resulting from too much sun that morning.

She dare not see him alone again, for she was afraid that he would take the opportunity to put to her the question he had meant to ask yesterday. As long as he never made his indecent proposal—never actually said the words—she could tell herself that his grandfather might have been wrong.

She and Lady Feather discussed the possibility of having their evening meal sent to their rooms; however, after considering all the speculation their continued absence would raise, especially since they meant to leave the following day, they decided to put in one final appearance. When the dinner gong sounded, they went down together, arm in arm.

Nor surprisingly, when they reached the music room Mrs. Quick was berating one of her daughters. "Mind your posture, young lady. If I have told you once, I have told you a million times, gentlemen do not look favorably upon females who slouch."

Though the object of this censure probably did not appreciate receiving the reprimand, Juliet was happy to hear it, for it meant that so far none of the Portman gentlemen had arrived. Even Mrs. Quick had sufficient social graces to realize that she must save her harangues for her family's ears only.

She must have realized as well that she could not ask her hostess why she had absented herself from the dinner table last evening. None the less, her curiosity was evident. After replying to Lady Featherstone's coolly polite greeting, she watched the older lady cross to the far end of the room and seat herself in a lone wing chair, where it would be impossible for anyone at the near end of the room to engage her in conversation without shouting.

Following her ladyship's example, Juliet crossed the fleur-de-lis carpet to join Beatrice Quick on the settee beside the fireplace. Situated as the two young ladies were, Juliet had no worry about Alex approaching her, for to do so would look most particular and would give rise to conjecture regarding his intentions.

And he could not have that! Not one of the Portman grandsons. Not when the lady was someone's natural daughter.

Juliet had only just taken her seat when Lord Bevin
entered the music room. To his credit, the old gentleman went directly to Lady Feather and bowed over
her hand, speaking softly to her, his words for her
ears only. It was not to be wondered at that the members of the Quick family found this unconventional
greeting odd, though they kept their opinions to themselves, merely watching the tête-à-tête as though it
were a play enacted for their entertainment.

Juliet watched as well. Aware as she was of the
conversation that had passed between those two old
friends yesterday evening, she assumed that his lordship was attempting to offer Lady Feather an apology
for offending her. Obviously, he made a bad job of it,
or else he chose not to apologize for the opinion he
had voiced regarding Juliet's unsuitability for either
of his grandsons. Whatever the cause, Lady Feather
withdrew her hand as quickly as possible, without uttering so much as a single word.

Alex and Tony arrived several minutes later, laughing at some private jest. Their smiles faded fast, however, when they became aware of the aura of coolness
that permeated the room. Because their grandfather
was clearly miffed at having his apology rejected, he
insisted they all go into the dining room immediately.

Mr. Claude Quick, not perceptive at the best of times,
took exception to this abrupt order to quit the music
room. "I say, Bevin. Bad show, old fellow, not offering
a man even one glass of sherry before dinner."

His host merely glared at him, then offered Mrs.
Quick his arm so they might proceed to the dining
room. If the other guests felt the loss of the aperitif,
they remained silent on the subject.

The meal that followed this inauspicious beginning

was as strained as any Juliet had ever endured, though Tony tried his best to engage each of the three younger females in conversation. Beatrice and Celeste, never at their best when in the presence of their mother, answered him shyly, while Juliet's replies to his sallies gave a new meaning to the word *brevity*.

The dessert course had barely arrived at the table before Lady Feather rose and suggested the ladies leave the gentlemen to their port. Five minutes later, while Beatrice and Celeste busied themselves searching through the available sheet music to see if there was something new they might play once the gentlemen joined them, Lady Feather bowed to Mrs. Quick and bid her a good evening.

"Juliet, my dear," she said, "come with me if you please, for I have need of you."

Since this little charade had been agreed upon before she and Lady Feather went down to dinner, Juliet rose obediently and followed her ladyship from the room, sparing only a brief smile for the sisters, who looked totally confused.

Later that evening, long after the tall case clock at the end of the corridor had struck eleven, Juliet heard someone scratch at her door. From the stillness of the house, she sensed that the rest of the family and guests were asleep in their beds. All save Alex. She knew without looking who stood outside her bedchamber door, just as she knew without asking that he would not go away until she spoke with him.

Angry with him for putting her in this untenable position, she took time to light the candle beside her bed. She shoved her feet into her carpet slippers; then, unable to locate her flannel dressing gown, she grabbed the light wool blanket from the foot of the bed and threw the cover around her shoulders to cover her night rail.

As before, the door to the dressing room was ajar, so she walked softly, to keep from disturbing Morag. Before she reached for the handle, Juliet took a deep breath, hoping it would give her strength. It failed miserably, and with no other alternative, she eased open the door. "What do you want?" she asked, the words even less hospitable than she had intended.

"Still suffering from the headache, are we?"

"There is no 'we.' "

Ignoring her rudeness, Alex picked up the long, thick braid that lay across her right shoulder. "Perhaps this is the culprit. Could it be that you plaited it too tightly?" He followed that foolish question with a smile that Juliet felt certain had broken at least a hundred hearts throughout Europe. "I would be happy to loosen it for you," he drawled.

Annoyed to find herself responding to that soft drawl, she yanked the braid from his hand. "It is late, Alex. Why are you here?"

"I was worried about you. Something is going on in this house. What it is, I do not know, but—"

"Truly? I had not noticed anything amiss."

He scoffed, patent disbelief in every line of his body. "Do not play the fool, Juliet, for it is not your style. A person had only to be present at dinner tonight to realize that tempers were frayed and that emotions were being kept on a tight leash."

"And you lay this at my door?"

"Only indirectly. You and her ladyship did not come down last evening, this afternoon you claim the headache, and this evening you fled to your room as soon as the meal was finished. Call me misguided if you wish, but I have to wonder what part your meetings with *Monsieur* Du Monde played in yours and Lady Featherstone's indisposition."

He reached out and caught her hand, and though she attempted to break free of his grasp, he held on. "Do not pull away, Juliet, please."

When she ceased to struggle, he placed her hand over his heart, his own hand covering hers. "I should have accompanied you to the village today. I wanted to, believe me, for I do not trust *Monsieur* Du Monde."

"And your reasons?"

"You will say I have no basis for my suspicions, and you will be correct. Still, I did not like the idea of your meeting this stranger alone. I tried to ask you yesterday to allow me to go with you today, but I could not find the right words. Words that would not make you angry enough to refuse me out of hand. Now, I wish I had just blurted out my request, for it is clear that something has upset you."

*Refuse me out of hand.* He had said much those same words yesterday afternoon. Had that been what he wished to ask her, to be allowed to go with her to meet her father? Juliet strained to see his eyes, to discover in their depths if he was being truthful. From what she could see, he was hiding nothing. "Was that *all* you wished to ask me?"

"Was it not enough?"

Wanting desperately to believe him, she said, "Was there nothing else on your mind at that time, Alex? Something that did not involve my meeting with my father?"

He seemed surprised by her intensity. "Nothing else, I assure you."

*Nothing else.* What marvelous words!

Upon hearing that magical utterance, Juliet felt as though a heavy weight had been lifted from her spirit. She was glad that her hand was over Alex's heart, and not his over hers, for he would have felt the instant quickening of her pulses.

*He had not meant to make her an indecent proposal!*

That idea—as demoralizing as it was demeaning—had come from his grandfather, not from Alex.

Juliet wanted to kick herself for doubting him. And for doubting herself as well.

She was a lady, one whose reputation was unblemished, and in the fourteen years she had known and loved Alex, he had always treated her with respect. And though the facts of her birth were never far from her thoughts, not by word or gesture had Alex indicated that they were important to him. He had referred to her many times as his friend, and it would seem that those were his true sentiments.

Of course, now that her mind was not clouded by her emotions, she was obliged to admit that while he had not meant to make her an *indecent* proposal, neither had he meant to offer her any *other* sort of proposal!

Juliet had let her imagination run away with her on that score. Perhaps it was because she loved Alex so much, and though she knew a marriage between them was ineligible, it was still the thing she wanted most in the world.

Of course, she had help misconstruing Alex's intentions. Morag and Lady Feather had done their parts!

When Morag had filled her head with that nonsense about his having a *tendre* for her, Juliet had lost all sense of balance. No wonder she had left herself open to hurt. Had she not been deluding herself that Alex wanted to marry her, perhaps she would not have been so quick to believe that he wanted to make her his mistress.

The circumstances clear at last, she breathed a sigh of relief. That sigh must have made it sound as though she had removed the weight of the world from her shoulders, for Alex smiled at her, amusement and sympathy blended in his eyes. "Feel better now?"

"Much," she replied, returning his smile.

"I cannot say I understand what just happened here," he said, "but I am not such a fool as to look a gift horse in the mouth."

She chuckled. "Are you calling me a horse?"

He gave her hand a playful squeeze, then released it. "A filly perhaps. A pretty, brown-eyed filly."

As compliments go, it was hardly the stuff of which romantic legends were made; even so, Juliet felt a warmth spread throughout her body. She was still basking in that warmth when he said he had something else to ask her. "About tomorrow."

*Tomorrow?* Had he heard somehow that she and Lady Feather planned to leave Portman Park tomorrow? Before she could ask him what he had heard, he surprised her by asking if she had read the latest *Times* brought from town.

"No. Why? Did it contain important news?"

"Very. The *Northumberland* has landed at St. Helena Island at last."

For just a moment, she did not understand to what he referred; then, suddenly she realized just how self-absorbed she had been these past few days. The world had not stopped just because Juliet Moseby had suffered a disappointment. It had continued to turn on its axis, and life had gone on. "Napoleon!" she said. "He has begun his exile at last. What wonderful news."

"Wonderful, indeed. And to celebrate this great news, I have decided we should have another of those alfresco breakfasts. Only this time, it will be a simple affair down at the weir. Just you, me, Tony, and the sisters. No servants, no tables and chairs, and certainly none of the accoutrements of fine dining the *ton* find necessary."

Juliet sighed, wishing with all her heart that she were not leaving the next day. "It sounds delightful."

Caught up in his plans, Alex failed to hear the wistfulness in Juliet's tone, and he continued, unaware that she had not agreed to join the celebration. "Cook has promised to prepare a nuncheon we can eat with our fingers," he said. "And we will take a blanket and sit on the ground, because that is the way the brave soldiers who fought Bonaparte's men ate their meals."

As if only just noticing that she wore a blanket draped across her shoulders, Alex curled his fingers around the folds of the woolen material, where it touched either side of her neck. Immediately, Juliet ceased to breathe, for after the merest hesitation, he urged her forward, not stopping until her body was pressed close against his.

Juliet knew full well what he meant to do. If her woman's instincts were not enough to tell her everything she needed to know, the purposeful look in Alex's eyes left no doubts as to what he wanted. Thrilled to know that he still found her pleasing, she turned her face up to his.

He drew in a sharp breath. "Juliet, you . . ."

Whatever he had meant to say, he must have thought better of it, for after groaning low in his throat, he bent his head toward hers and kissed her. The kiss was slow and gloriously mind-numbing, but it was over much too soon, leaving Juliet breathless and longing for more.

"May I have this blanket?" he asked, his voice so husky she barely recognized it. "For tomorrow."

Though she made no reply, he slipped the blanket from around her and tossed it over his right shoulder, leaving her wearing nothing but her night rail. The candlelight was behind her, and it must have rendered the white lawn practically transparent, for Alex seemed unable to take his eyes off her. First he studied her face, then her neck, and finally he let his gaze travel slowly down to her toes and back again, apparently not missing a single curve in between.

While he looked her over, she stood there, unmoving, feeling the heat of his gaze as though it were a physical entity, feeling it and reveling in the sensation.

When he finished perusing every inch of her, he

drew in a ragged breath. "You are unbelievably beautiful," he said.

Juliet shivered, though it was his words and not the cool night air that affected her. Hoping for another kiss, she turned her face up to his once again.

To her surprise, he put his hands on her shoulders and gently pushed her back into the bedchamber, while he remained in the corridor, his hands behind his back as if he were afraid he might reach for her again. "Close the door," he ordered, almost as if he were angry with her.

"But, Alex, I—"

"Damnation, Juliet, do it now! While you still can. Before I lose my last shred of self-control."

"What about my blanket?"

"You can get another one," he said. He lifted the material to his nose and breathed deeply, as if savoring the scent of her that clung to the wool. "This one is mine."

# Chapter Twelve

*T*he next morning, Juliet realized she had failed to tell Alex that she and Lady Feather were leaving for Bath. Needing to inform him of that fact, and not wanting him to leave for the weir before she had the opportunity to tell him good-bye, she hurried down to the sunny yellow room set aside for those who wished to partake of a more substantial morning meal than tea and toast. Though a handsome oak sideboard contained at least a dozen covered dishes, the only person seated at the small, round table was Alex. He had finished his repast, for the footman who stood ready to serve him had already removed his plate and was pouring him a cup of tea.

"Will that be all, Major?"

"Yes, thank you. You may go—No, wait," Alex said, looking up to discover Juliet smiling at him. "It appears Miss Moseby has decided to give us the pleasure of her company."

After placing his napkin on the table, Alex stood, then came around to offer her a fresh plate. "May I serve you something? I can recommend the shaved ham. As for the currant buns, they are not to be missed."

"They sound delicious, but I had toast and chocolate an hour ago. If the tea is still hot, however, I would not refuse a cup."

Alex held a chair for her, and once she was seated, he waved the servant away and poured the tea for her himself. "If you are not hungry, Juliet, had you some other reason for coming to this room? I ask in a general way, mind you, for if I inquired if you had come to see me in *particular,* I daresay you would think me an egotist."

The corners of her pretty mouth twitched. "Do not be concerned on that score," she said, "for I have always thought you an egotist."

"Whereas I, madam, have always thought you much too free with your opinions."

"I know," she said. "It is part of my charm."

She attempted to hide her smile by raising the teacup to her lips, and Alex wondered, as she looked over the rim at him, if she had any idea how adorable she was. Or how much he wanted to take her in his arms and kiss that saucy mouth.

"As it happens," she said, setting the cup aside, "I did come in search of you, and for a very particular reason. I came to inform you of a decision that Lady Feather and I reached yesterday morning."

When she said this last, that enchanting will-o'-the-wisp smile disappeared, and Alex felt an unpleasant tightening in his solar plexus. Whatever it was that Juliet had come to tell him, he knew he was not going to like it.

"I regret that I cannot attend your celebration at the weir this afternoon, Alex, for it sounds most enjoyable. Unfortunately, Lady Feather and I are leaving Portman Park this morning."

Leaving! No. He did not like this news one little bit. "When you say 'leaving,' are you referring to your planned removal to Auntie's Cottage?"

She shook her head. "We mean to quit Hampshire entirely."

"I knew it!"

Alex bit back a curse. He had known all along that

something was going on in that house, especially after the previous night's dinner, when the tension at the table was so thick he fancied he could reach out and touch it. "When I asked you last night if your meetings with *Monsieur* Du Monde had played any part in yours and Lady Featherstone's unaccountable indisposition the evening before, you vowed that they had not."

"And I spoke the truth."

"Forgive me, Juliet, but I know of nothing else that would account for this strain in a house where once there was only friendship."

"My father played no part in what occurred here last evening or the evening before. Upon this you have my word of honor."

As though reluctant to say more, she used the tip of her finger to trace the raised design in the damask cloth covering the table. When she returned her attention to Alex, he saw regret in her eyes for what she was about to reveal. "Her ladyship's behavior, and mine as well, stem from something that happened between Lady Feather and your grandfather."

Alex could not believe his ears. "But they have been friends for more than forty years. Surely my grandfather would never—" He stopped, for a sudden angry flash in her eyes told him that he was about to make a serious blunder. Damnation! "What on earth did Grandfather do?"

"It was something he said. An insult that Lady Feather took very much to heart."

"An insult? But what could he have said to put a wedge between two such old friends?"

She looked down at her teacup, and if the blush that stained her cheeks was any indication, she found this conversation embarrassing in the extreme. "I beg of you, Alex, do not ask me anything more. Theirs was a private conversation, and it must remain so until one of them chooses to make it public."

Judging by the determined tone of Juliet's voice, she had no intention of divulging more, and Alex was obliged to let the matter rest; at least until he could find his grandfather and demand to know what had come over him. He knew the old gentleman was very proud, and he could be quite stiff-rumped at times; especially if someone acted in a way that went counter to his own firmly held opinions. But this was incomprehensible. How could his grandfather throw away a friendship that had sustained him through the devastating loss of his wife, and later through the accidental death of his daughter-in-law and his only son?

Though frustrated at this unexpected turn of events, Alex knew Juliet well enough to realize there was nothing he could say to dissuade her from leaving. She was completely loyal to Lady Featherstone—understandably so— and where her ladyship went, Juliet went. It was as simple as that.

"Where do you mean to go?"

"We have decided to spend some time in Bath. If we find the society there to our liking, we may purchase one of the town houses on the Royal Crescent."

Relieved to discover that their destination was the popular spa town, Alex was struck by a sudden and very promising idea. "Here's a thought," he said. "Bridborne Grange, the estate I inherited recently, is in Dorset, probably no more than thirty-five or forty miles south of Bath. I should hate to desert my grandfather without sufficient notice, but if you will agree to remain at the Park for another day or two, it would be my pleasure to escort you ladies to Bath."

For an instant, he thought she would agree to the change in plan, but before he could say more, she shook her head. "Thank you, Alex, but my father has offered us the use of his traveling chaise, and he has already made the arrangements, including putting his coachman at our disposal. As well, to insure our safety he has seen to the hiring of a pair of outriders. I cannot refuse him now, not after he has gone to all this trouble.''

Faced with a fait accompli, Alex added efficiency to the growing list of the Frenchman's crimes. "It would appear that *Monsieur* Du Monde has thought of everything.''

"He has, indeed. All that remains for me to do is to see to the proper stowing of our trunks aboard the carriage.''

"Do not give that another thought, for my valet can see to it for you. Ottway is a man of many talents, and you can leave the details to him.''

One detail, at least, Alex obviously meant to take care of himself, for after a minute or two of silence— minutes in which Juliet resorted to drinking cold tea rather than look to see if he cared where she went— he came around the table and took her hands, obliging her to stand.

When she looked up into his blue-gray eyes, she saw something there, something she had never seen before. Too unsure of herself to put a name to what she saw, she merely allowed him to bring both her hands to his lips, then watched speechlessly as he planted soft, tantalizing kisses on her wrists, on her palms, and on each finger in turn.

"Fourteen kisses," he said. "They will have to suffice until we meet again.''

"Oh?'' Her voice nearly failed her. "Will we meet again?''

"Of course.''

There was no "of course'' about it!

Before she could ask him when he thought a meeting likely, he continued to speak, almost as if thinking aloud. "I will probably leave Portman Park within the next two days. There will be traveling time to consider, then I will remain a sennight to ten days at Bridborne Grange, just to get a feel for the place and to see what needs doing immediately. If all goes well, I should reach Bath within the fortnight."

"Are . . . are you coming to Bath?"

"Of course."

*Of course.* There were those two words again, and with them, Juliet's heart began to beat dangerously fast.

"The idea of traveling to the spa town had not previously crossed my mind," he said. "But a few minutes ago, while we were talking, I began to think there might be an attraction or two in Bath that I would not want to miss."

Juliet had no idea how to respond to the information. She knew how it made her feel—unbelievably happy—and she knew what she wanted it to mean—that the attraction he was coming to see was *her.* But what if she was wrong? Anyone might come to a popular place like Bath.

Still, he had kissed her hands fourteen times. Juliet found that very encouraging, though it was possible she might be reading more into his proposed visit than it warranted. Afraid to trust her instincts, she said nothing, merely waited to hear what he would say next.

Unfortunately, they were interrupted by Lord Bevin's valet with word that his lordship wished to see Major Portman in his bedchamber as soon as possible. "If you please, sir, there is a matter he wishes to discuss with you."

Alex told the servant he would be up directly, then he returned his attention to Juliet. "I have no idea what my grandfather wants, but I feel I must go. Especially if I am to leave here shortly."

He crossed the room, but stopped at the door. When he turned back to look at her, the smile on his face was so beguiling it obliged Juliet to catch hold of the chair to steady herself. "Under no circumstances," he said, "are you to set one foot off this estate before I have given you a proper good-bye."

"No, no. I would not think of it."

*A proper good-bye.* She had no idea what such a parting entailed, but merely thinking of the possibilities left her feeling tingly all over.

He quit the room, closing the door behind him, while Juliet remained standing beside the table, assimilating everything Alex had said and done. She was coming to a most promising conclusion regarding his actions, and their effect upon her future, when she heard the rattle of the traveling chaise coming down the carriageway. Curious to see what sort of coach her father kept, she hurried toward the vestibule, not suspecting for an instant that within five minutes of arriving outside, her world would be shattered into a million pieces.

Ottway, true to his reputation as a man of many talents, had set two of Lord Bevin's strongest footmen the task of taking the ladies' trunks belowstairs and delivering them to the carriageway. Once that business was seen to, he visited the kitchen to procure a jug of lemonade and a box of cakes and sandwiches, in case the ladies and their maids found themselves in need of refreshments before they stopped for the night. He was consulting the atlas in his lordship's bookroom, to discover the best route for the coachman to take, when he heard the rattle of the carriage wheels.

Having learned what he needed to know, Ottway closed the atlas and exited the bookroom by way of the French windows. Hurrying around to the pleached avenue, he reached the carriageway just as the coachman reined in the four spirited horses. "Whoa!" the driver called, stopping the team not far from where the ladies' trunks stood.

The two outriders had remained beside the stuccoed

arch of the walled entrance, probably to avoid being called upon to help load the trunks. But another rider—a gentleman, judging by the excellent cut of his coat and pantaloons—encouraged his horse to continue up the carriageway.

By this time Miss Moseby, a very nice young lady in Ottway's opinion, had joined him. "What nonsense is this?" she asked.

For an instant, the valet had thought the question was meant for him, but upon discovering that the lady was looking toward the dower house that Major Portman insisted upon calling a cottage, he relaxed. To Ottway's surprise, strolling toward them, as though he had not a care in the world, was none other than Captain Geofrey Lansdale.

Ottway hadn't seen the captain in more than a week, not since that night in London when the military gentleman had sustained a brutal beating at the hands of a pair of thugs, minions of a gambler reported to be as evil as they come. And the way Ottway remembered it, the captain was supposed to be in hiding from that evil individual.

Miss Moseby must have been under the same impression, for she walked purposefully toward the captain, meeting him halfway between the cottage and the pleached avenue. "Sir," she said, "what are you doing out of doors, where anyone might see you?"

The captain lifted his hat in salute. "Today is a very special day, Miss Moseby, and I do not mean to spend it holed up in an attic like some frightened squirrel. Not when there is a celebration being held down at the weir. I spent eight years chasing Boney's men from Hades and back, and I insist upon my share of the jubilation at that curst Frenchman's exile."

Juliet smiled in sympathy, perfectly understanding his feelings, imprudent though they were. "Celebration or no, Captain Lansdale, I do not believe it is at

all wise for you to risk being seen. And if Alex were
here, I am persuaded he would agree with me."

"There he is now," the captain said, pointing toward
the pleached avenue, where a handsome gentleman
dressed in a sportsman's hunting jacket and dun-
colored trousers had just come into sight. "Let us ask
him what he thinks."

"Sorry," Juliet said, "but that is not Alex. It is
Tony."

"You don't say so!" Clearly impressed by her certainty, Captain Lansdale asked her how she could tell
one twin from the other. "As like as two peas if you
ask me."

"Not at all, Captain. In fact—"

Juliet stopped abruptly, for she had only just noticed
that the gentleman riding up the carriageway was not
one of the outriders. "Oh, sir," she said, lifting her
hand in greeting, "I did not expect to see you again."

Francois Du Monde reigned in his horse just a few
feet from where Juliet chatted with a slender young
man. Touching his riding crop to the brim of his hat,
he bid her a good morning. "I hope you are not annoyed with me for coming here, Juliet, but I wished
to see for myself that all was in order for your departure. If anything is not as you would like it, you have
only to say the word, and I will—"

He almost choked on the words so quickly swallowed, for a gentleman wearing hunting attire had
joined Juliet and the other young man, and they had
all turned to look up at him, giving him an unimpeded
view of their faces. *"Nom de Dieu!"* he gasped.

He could not believe his ill luck, for the two men
standing on either side of his daughter were none
other than Captain Geofrey Lansdale and Mr. Anthony Portman.

"Worldly!" Lansdale said. "How the deuce did you
find me?"

Du Monde ignored the question, for his only concern was his daughter, whose brown eyes reflected her confusion.

"Captain," she said, "being out in the sunshine after so many days indoors must be affecting your vision, for I fear you have made a mistake. This gentleman is Monsieur *Francois Du Monde*."

The captain made a snarling sound deep in his throat, then stepped toward Du Monde, his hands balled into fists as if he meant to use them as weapons. "Francois Du Monde, is it?" He spat on the ground, as though merely saying the name left a bad taste in his mouth. "Francois Du Monde or Frank Worldly, a villain by any other name is still a villain."

Juliet looked at the captain as though she thought he had lost his mind, then she stepped toward the horse, her hands reaching up to take Du Monde's. "Sir. I pray you will forgive this very odd behavior. My friend meant no harm, I assure you. It is just that he recently sustained an injury, and he—"

"No!" Anthony Portman yelled, grabbing Juliet by the arm and yanking her back, forcing her to release Du Monde's hands. "Do not touch that scoundrel, Juliet. He is a viper, merely disguised as a man."

"Scoundrel? Viper?" By now, tears filled Juliet's eyes, and her voice quivered with uncertainty.

Seeing her like this, and fearing that any moment she might turn from him, Du Monde felt a sudden hollowness inside his chest. Damn the fates for prompting him to ride here this morning. And damn those two young jackanapes! If he had brought his sword stick, instead of this blasted riding crop, he would now be turning it red with their blood. "Juliet," he said, "allow me to explain."

"Do not speak to her," Portman said.

"Tony, please," Juliet said, "let him explain. This is all some horrible mistake. It must be."

"It is no mistake," Portman said. "Believe me, Juliet, I know. The man you called Du Monde is none other than Frank Worldly, the most despised villain in London."

# Chapter Thirteen

*J*uliet felt as if some icy hand had wrapped itself around her heart, freezing her into immobility.

*Du Monde.* If she had given a thought to even the most basic French lessons learned at Miss Trillium's Female Academy in Brighton, she would have recalled that *du monde* translated to "of the world." Worldly. An appropriate name for the sort of person who thought nothing of having a man beaten within an inch of his life for not paying his gambling debts.

She looked toward Captain Lansdale, knowing the pain he had suffered because of just such a beating. The first day she saw him, he had been lying on that cot in the attic, his head swathed in a bandage and his lower lip split and swollen. When he had attempted even the simplest movements, he had been obliged to wrap his arms around his aching ribs, his eyes closed against the pain.

Juliet had felt such sympathy for him. Now, remembering that day, nausea rose in her throat, all but choking her, for it had been her father who ordered that done to Geofrey Lansdale.

Her father, *Monsieur* Francois Du Monde.

She stared at the man on the horse, wondering just what sort of person he was. What sort of monster? Who was this man her mother had loved enough to bear him a child?

He had betrayed them both—her and her mother. He had left her mother to endure the shame of ostracism from her family as well as her friends; it mattered not that he claimed to have been in a carriage accident that kept him from reaching the church in time for the wedding. The result was the same for Dora Moseby—disgrace in the eyes of the world.

As for Juliet, Du Monde had betrayed her by burrowing beneath the carefully constructed wall that had been her protection since childhood. He had won her trust, convinced her that she could lower her guard and perhaps one day come to love him as a daughter loves a father. And all the time he had hidden from her his true nature.

And the truth was, that he was a villain.

*Villain. Villain. Villain.*

The word echoed inside her brain until her temples throbbed with pain. Slowly, the carriage, the horses, everything and everyone in Juliet's line of vision grew wavy and began to fade. She knew she was about to faint, but there was nothing she could do to prevent it. Fortunately, as she felt herself sinking toward the ground, she was caught and lifted in a pair of strong arms.

As her rescuer turned and began walking toward the house, the last thing Juliet heard was her father's voice. "You!" he shouted. "Lansdale. You will pay for this day's work. And this time you will pay with your life!"

Thankfully, Juliet heard no more, for blackness descended upon her, blocking out all sound, all thought, all pain.

She must have been unconscious for only a matter of seconds, for when she opened her eyes, she saw the dome-like, interlaced beech branches overhead and knew she was being carried down the pleached avenue, her head resting on a very masculine shoulder. "You are safe," Alex said, "I have you."

Alex? When had he come outside? Juliet had no recollection of his arrival. Had he heard everything? Did he know who her father was? Had he been there to witness her disgrace? She groaned, and Alex leaned his cheek against her forehead, crooning soft nonsense into her ear.

"Close your eyes," he said, "and do not think of anything. You will be in your bedchamber in a matter of seconds, and Morag can give you something to make you sleep. When you wake, this will be over."

She groaned again, for she knew it would never be over, not her relationship to Du Monde, and certainly not the irreparable harm such a connection would inflict upon the rest of her life. She had gone looking for her father—it was all her doing, the opening of this Pandora's box.

Her father was who he was, the sort of man decent people despised, and the world would never forget that he was the tree from which Juliet had sprung. He was an evil man, and that fact alone had put paid to any chance she and Alex may have had.

If Lord Bevin had thought Juliet Moseby, nameless bastard, was unworthy of his grandson, she did not even want to *think* about what his opinion would be of her a few minutes from now, when he heard who her father was. Once he knew the worst, his lordship might well order Juliet from his home, then forbid his grandsons ever to speak her name again.

Less than an hour ago, in the sunny yellow room where Alex had broken his fast, he had made Juliet hope that they might have a future together. Now, of course, she knew that all such hope was gone. Even if Alex loved her as she loved him, she could never marry him. His was an old and respected name, and she would not besmirch it by linking it with that of a man known throughout the country as a vicious criminal.

Alex had carried her up the stone stairs with little

physical effort. Unfortunately, when he reached her bed and laid her down very gently, Juliet was obliged to expend a great deal of mental effort. Unshed tears clogged her throat, and it was all she could do not to cling to him and beg him to stay with her just a few minutes longer.

"Take care of her," he said, his hand on Morag's shoulder. "She has sustained a shock."

He left her then, telling Morag that he needed to go back outside to see what he could do to ensure his friend's safety. "I will be back," he said.

When he closed the door behind him, Juliet whispered, "Goodbye, my love." Then she turned her face to the wall and cried as she had not cried since her mother died, fourteen years before.

As instructed, Morag prepared for Juliet a tisane sparingly laced with laudanum, and Juliet, too distressed to argue that she did not wish to be drugged, drank every drop of it. As a result, she slept for the next six hours. When she awoke, feeling as though her head had been stuffed with cotton wool, it was late afternoon.

Her bedchamber, which had been stripped of all her personal items that morning, now looked much as it had for the past fortnight. Her comb and brush were on the dressing table, and her carpet slippers and dressing gown were in front of the fire, soaking up warmth in case she wished to get out of bed. Morag sat beside the fire as well, her mending basket at her feet and a partially hemmed handkerchief lying forgotten across her knee.

"Morag?"

"I'm here, lass."

The Scotswoman put aside her sewing and hurried over to the bed, concern making her face appear more drawn and tired than Juliet had ever seen it. "You're awake at last, are you. Well, healing sleep is what you needed."

"I am awake," Juliet said, her voice husky with sleep and despair, "though I cannot see that sleeping healed anything. Unless, of course, it was all a bad dream, and my father was not here after all."

"Nay, lass. That was no dream."

Try as she would, Juliet could not keep the tears from pooling in her eyes. "Oh, Morag, I should have listened to you. You said he was the devil incarnate, and you were right."

"Yes, I was right, but I dinna take comfort in the fact."

Juliet put her hands to her temples, wishing that wooly feeling inside her head would go away so she could think straight. "The trouble with being drugged," she said, "is that when you wake, the problems are still there. Only by then you are so muddle-headed you cannot think what to do about them."

"It's a good thing, then, that there are others available to do the thinking for you. At least for today."

Never able to let others assume her burdens, Juliet looked around the room, as if that might clear her mind, and spied her trunk pushed into a far corner. "I suppose I shall have to hire a coach after all for the trip to Bath."

Suddenly remembering that Lady Feather had wanted to leave Portman Park immediately, Juliet felt a fresh wave of guilt wash over her. "Was her ladyship upset at having to remain here another night?"

"She was far more concerned about your distress than about her own inconvenience. As is no more than one would expect, for she is a lady through and through. Which is more than can be said for *some* people in this house."

Juliet moaned. "Mrs. Quick?"

"Aye. The she-devil."

"I can just imagine what she had to say about me."

Morag shook her head. "I hope you cannot, lass, for it was as mean-spirited as anything I have ever heard."

"Poor Lady Feather, to be obliged to listen to such vitriol."

"Well, as to that, from what I was told by one of the footmen as heard it all through the drawing room door, Lady Featherstone did a mite more talking than listening. Called the woman a vulgar fishwife, did her ladyship, and more besides."

"Please," Juliet said, pulling the cover over her head, "I do not want to hear any more."

"Then you rest a bit longer, lass, and give that muddleheaded feeling a chance to go away. Meanwhile, I'll go belowstairs and see to getting you a mite of broth and some tea."

"I am not hungry."

"That's as may be, but you'll need your strength, I'm thinking, for whatever the rest of the day may bring."

Just before she exited the room, Morag remembered something she had meant to say earlier. "By the way, Miss Juliet, one of the servants from Stone House brought over a packet addressed to you. Came all the way from London, it did. I put it there, on the bedside table so you wouldn't miss it."

"A soldier needs his strength to get through the day," Ottway said, setting his knife and fork across his plate, then making a show of patting his full stomach. "And if they'd served food this tasty in the army, Mrs. Upjohn, I vow, we'd have beaten old Boney's men in half the time."

The innkeeper's wife smiled her pleasure at the compliment and lifted her glass in toast to her guest. "I am a good cook, if I do say so as shouldn't, but ye'd never know it around this place."

While the major and Mr. Anthony Portman had gone around to the front of the Blue Lion to see what they could discover about Francois Du Monde from Cyrus Upjohn, the innkeeper, Ottway had gone around to the back and presented himself to the innkeeper's wife at the kitchen door. Explaining to the thin, tired-looking woman who was both cook and maid of all work that he was the type who liked to eat his mutton in a kitchen, the Welshman pressed a shilling into her work-roughened hand. "This be for you, missus, for your trouble."

She had served his plate with beef and boiled potatoes, and brought the bottle of gin he ordered to wash it down. He was not surprised when she accepted his invitation to bring an extra glass and join him at the table.

What followed the first glass of gin was a series of complaints from the woman to go along with his meal.

"Never tell me," Ottway said, topping off the woman's glass, "that your husband be the thickheaded sort who doesn't know how to appreciate a good woman."

"Appreciate me?" She displayed a large and very recent bruise on her forearm. "Treats me like a slave, he does. And never so much as a farthing do I get to spend on myself."

Ottway *tsk-tsk*ed, his tone sympathetic.

"Not a farthing," the woman repeated, downing the entire contents of her glass, then looking longingly toward the half-empty bottle.

Ottway filled her glass again, this time to the top, then while she drank passed two more coins across the scarred deal table. "Perhaps your husband doesn't have a farthing to spare."

"Ha! Got a leather pouch full of guineas, he has. Got it from that Frenchman what were staying here the past few days."

Ottway yawned, feigning boredom. "Frenchmen.

I've no use for them myself. On account of the war, you understand."

"Right you are," Mrs. Upjohn said, emptying her glass, then pushing it toward him for another refill. When Ottway obliged, she sat back in her chair, apparently not finished with her story. "My husband don't like the Frenchies neither, but he did that monsewer's bidding fast enough when he saw that pouch of guineas. Even got a couple of the 'gentlemen' to help him."

She looked around her to be certain no one had come into the kitchen without her knowing it. "Smugglers, I'm talking about," she whispered. "Two of 'em, big they was, came and did a job for the monsewer t'other day, and my husband did the paying of 'em." Her voice regained its volume and its whine. "He paid 'em only half what the Frenchman gave him in that leather pouch. Then he hid the pouch so I couldn't find it, he did."

Ottway slid another shilling across the table. "What sort of job did the 'gentlemen' do?"

"Don't know for sure," she said, the last word coming out noticeably slurred. "This I can tell you, though. When the monsewer come back to the inn that day, asking Upjohn to find someone to do a job, the look of hatred on his face were such that it fair froze the blood in my veins." She took a large swallow of gin, as if to rid herself of the memory. "That night, Zeke Dobbs were beat up something fierce."

Alex was not the least bit surprised that Ottway learned so much. The Welshman had a way of getting people to talk, and Alex was just glad that he had gleaned so much.

As for his and his brother's inquiry, it had yielded little. Upjohn claimed to know nothing, except that Du Monde had paid his shot at the inn, then sent his carriage back to London empty. "He kept the saddle horse hired from the blacksmith," the innkeeper said, "but where he went is a real mystery, it is."

"A likely story," Tony said later, after tossing a coin to the stable lad who brought around the curricle. "Worldly is hiding somewhere, mark my word, just waiting until the time is right to make good on his threat against Lansdale."

"If smugglers be involved," Ottway said, once he was certain the lad had returned to the stable, "the Frenchman could be any place. The 'gentlemen' like to keep their routes quiet-like."

Alex considered this information for a time. He really did not care where Du Monde took himself off to, as long as he never came near Juliet, Lansdale, or Portman Park again.

"What should we do with this other information, Major? Should the local beadle be told about the Frenchman being behind the beating of the baker?"

That question was easy for Alex to answer. "Whatever a bully like Zeke Dobbs did to anger Du Monde is no concern of mine. Nor is his present state of health."

"My sentiments exactly," Tony said. "As for telling the beadle, the man is a strutting rooster, full of his own importance, and as near to ineffectual as makes no difference. As long as Du Monde's threat against Captain Lansdale remains only a threat, then I believe we would do well to keep this entire affair to ourselves."

Alex agreed, for keeping Geofrey Lansdale safe was only one of his objectives. The other was to keep Juliet's name from being bandied about.

"What of the outriders the Frenchman hired to escort the carriage?" Ottway said. "They saw and heard everything. Will they be willing to keep such likely gossip to themselves, do you think? Or will they be bruiting this entire business about?"

Alex cast an involuntary glance at his right hand,

which was surprisingly rough-looking, with the skin across the knuckles broken and a new bruise beginning to show color. "My brother and I had a little talk with the outriders, and I do not think they will be spreading any tales about Miss Moseby."

"The truth has a way of coming out, Major."

"True. But at least those two will not enjoy telling it."

"Then let's hope that be an end to it. For the captain's sake and for the young lady's."

Juliet might have been pleased to know that Alex and Tony were looking out for her interests, had she not been so totally overset by the information in the packet sent to her by the Bow Street runner, Mr. Wister Yarborough, information about the life and career of Francois Du Monde, also known as Frank Worldly. "Why," she asked, the word little more than a moan, "could I not have received this packet before I agreed to that first meeting in the village?"

With trembling hands, she read through the neatly written sheets a second time, receiving at last the answers to her questions concerning the runner's initial, rather cryptic letter. From the beginning, she had questioned Wister Yarborough's choice of words. He had mentioned "hindrances" and "unlooked-for difficulties" in his original search for her father. Now, of course, he made her aware in sickening detail of the men who guarded Francois Du Monde, ruffians who threatened the runner with bodily harm if he did not desist in his inquiry into their employer's private life and business.

As for the people he had questioned, they had revealed little except their abject fear of the man known as Frank Worldly. One thing, at least, was clear: that he owned the house in which he held his gaming hell. How he came by the funds to purchase the house was something no one wished to discuss. "Obviously," the runner stated, "he used proceeds from whatever hocus-pocus occupation he had followed during the years following his association with your mother."

*Hocus-pocus.* Juliet shuddered. More euphemisms meant to hide the full ugliness of his criminal lifestyle.

What the runner *did* disclose was a brief summary of Du Monde's life during the past quarter century.

*I did manage to discover that Du Monde, was not always the sort of man he is today. In his early years, he had been both honest and sincere in his desire to become a painter. Unfortunately, the change in his status from aristocratic and wealthy young Frenchman to "tolerated" emigre soon had an effect upon his personality and his ambitions.*

*While still professing his desire to become a painter, he actually became part of a family business involving supplying the army quartermasters with poorly made boots. There were also whispers about Du Monde and his cousin spying for their previous homeland, but I found no actual proof to substantiate those allegations.*

*Following a carriage accident that may or may not have been retribution for having diddled his cousin out of his share of some side activity, Du Monde spent three years in Newgate Prison. Rumor has it that this, too, was a result of his cousin's continued animosity.*

*Upon his release from Newgate, Du Monde was, by all accounts, a very bitter man. Disowned by his family, and feeling himself betrayed by them, he began using the name Worldly.*

*My advice to you, Miss Moseby, is that you
have as little as possible to do with this man.*

"Fine advice," Juliet said, crumpling the pages into
a ball and throwing them onto the embers remaining
in the fireplace. "Unfortunately, it comes a bit late to
be of any use to me."

The paper caught fire quickly, flaring into bright
orange and blue flames, but as soon as it burned itself
out, with nothing remaining but bits of black ash, she
turned away and went to her dressing table, where she
began anew her plans to leave Portman Park the next
morning. Before she left, however, she felt she needed
to apologize to Captain Lansdale for the beating he
took at her father's instigation. With that objective
in mind, she asked Morag if the captain was still at
Auntie's Cottage.

"As far as I know, he's still there. Master Tony told
that valet of his, him as thinks so highly of himself, to
see to moving the captain's traps to the house. But
then, Master Tony and the major left right away for
the village, and so far, Mr. Eisner hasn't bestirred
himself."

"I am happy that is the case," Juliet said, "for there
is something I must say to the captain. I feel honor-
bound to speak to him, to beg his forgiveness for
bringing my father to—for bringing *Monsieur* Du
Monde to Portman Park. Naturally, I should much
prefer to speak to Captain Lansdale at the cottage,
where we will not be overheard."

From the pinched look around Morag's mouth, she
did not approve of this idea; however, she kept her
opinion to herself. Without uttering a word, she
fetched a peach-colored frock that was not too badly
wrinkled from having been packed, a pair of half
boots, and a tan spencer, and began helping Juliet
dress.

"You can go out the front way if you want to, Miss Juliet, for there will be none belowstairs save the servants. As for the she-devil, she has already gone to her bedchamber to dress for dinner. As have Miss Celeste and Miss Beatrice—the young lady as came by earlier to ask how you were feeling."

Returning to the subject of Mrs. Quick, Morag said, "With only two days left of their proposed stay, I wager the she-devil is getting nervous about their chances of ever catching Master Tony in parson's mousetrap. Wouldn't surprise me at all to hear that she's berating the poor young ladies right this minute for their failures. Probably planning to regale them in all their finery tonight."

Juliet's thoughts were on what she would say to Captain Lansdale, so she paid little attention to Morag's gossipy monologue, except for the part about there being no one belowstairs. As soon as she was dressed, she hurried from the bedchamber, descended the stone stairs, passed through the vestibule, and left the house, all without meeting a soul. Grateful for that bit of good fortune, she had just come to the end of the pleached avenue where it met the carriageway when she noticed a canvas-draped farm wagon pulled by two horses stopped just in front of the cottage.

Strange, she thought, that Eisner should need a wagon just to transport a valise the half mile from the cottage to the house.

That thought had no more than passed through her brain when the door to the cottage burst open, and two men wearing the rough trousers and leather smocks of common laborers came outside, dragging something between them. To Juliet's horror, that *thing* was Geofrey Lansdale.

Juliet gasped, for ropes bound the captain at his hands and his feet, and a cloth was tied tightly over his mouth. Though he struggled to break free, he was no match for the two burly men, who lifted him like a sack of grain and tossed him into the back of the waiting wagon.

Shock rendered Juliet as immobile as a statue, and while she watched the scene being enacted before the cottage, one man jumped in the wagon bed and covered the captain completely with the canvas. The other fellow climbed up on the plank seat, gathered up the reins and a whip, then hit the lead horse a savage blow across its haunch. The poor animal jerked to a start, and then the team took off toward the wall. Mere seconds later, the wagon holding the kidnappers and Captain Lansdale had passed through the arched entrance and disappeared down the lane, with nothing remaining but a cloud of dust raised in their rush to be gone.

Freed at last from her paralysis, Juliet found her voice. "Help! Help!'

When no one came to her immediate aid, she realized that she had to act quickly before the wagon got too far away. Picking up her skirts, she ran toward the stables, where two grooms had just appeared in the doorway, obviously coming in answer to her call. One of them held a pitchfork in his hand. "What's amiss?" he asked.

"Saddle my mare," Juliet ordered the one who spoke. "And you," she said to another, "run up to the house and tell your master that Captain Lansdale has been kidnapped, and that I mean to follow the men who took him."

"But miss, you're not dressed for riding. Besides, twilight be just around the corner, and I'm sure Lord Bevin would not approve of—"

"Go!" she shouted. "There is no time to argue."

Without another word, he touched his forelock and ran to deliver her message.

The moment the first groom brought Princess out,

Juliet bid him toss her into the saddle. "When Major Portman arrives," she said, "inform him that the wagon carrying Captain Lansdale turned in the direction of the New Forest."

"Yes, miss."

The mare, eager for a bit of exercise, took off at a canter down the carriageway, obliging Juliet to yell her parting remark over her shoulder. "Tell the major that I will follow the kidnappers as closely as I dare."

She said no more, for Princess had already changed to a gallop, and for better or worse, off horse and rider sped in pursuit of the farm wagon.

Within minutes she was behind them, following the trail of dust raised by the speeding wagon, and staying as close as possible to them without being seen.

The kidnappers were, in fact, headed for the New Forest. Furthermore, it appeared that their destination was that secluded area where the Portman party had eaten their alfresco breakfast several days ago, for the driver turned the horses off the lane onto the same narrow track.

Unlike that previous pleasure trip from Portman Park to the New Forest, this ride took less than half an hour. For this, at least, Juliet was grateful, for the sun had already begun to set, and she knew that the smears of yellow and orange in the distant sky would soon give way to twilight's purplish blue. Already the tall, thick trees on either side of the track blocked out most of the light, obliging Juliet to slow Princess to a walk or risk the mare stepping into a hole.

Twilights were short-lived in the forest, and once the light failed completely, Juliet would be forced to give up her pursuit of the wagon and return to the lane to wait for whoever came to her aid.

Even now, she could not see the wagon ahead of her, so she used the rattle of the wheels as her guide. The instant the sound of the wagon stopped, so did

Juliet. After several minutes, when the wagon did not move again, Juliet dismounted and wrapped the mare's reins around the low-hanging limb of a birch tree.

She had a pretty good idea why the kidnappers had come to this place. Unless she missed her guess, they meant to make use of the deep ditch that had once been a popular route for smugglers moving contraband. The ditch ran northward for at least twenty miles, and southward to the sea for at least ten miles. Once inside that ditch, the kidnappers would be virtually hidden from sight, and they would be almost impossible to follow in the dark.

If only Alex would arrive!

Wanting to assure herself that she had guessed correctly about the men using the ditch, Juliet moved forward slowly and quietly on foot, going from one wide-boled tree to another, taking care to remain hidden whenever possible. At the sound of voices, she ducked beneath an ancient low-growing hazel, lying flat on the ground.

"Here he be," said a man with a nasally twang in his voice. "Show him, Ned."

At the *whoosh*ing sound of the canvas being thrown back, Juliet rose up on her elbows so she could peek beneath the foliage. From her vantage point, she watched as the two men lifted Captain Lansdale out of the wagon and tossed him none too gently onto the ground. The captain moaned, and immediately Juliet heard a muttered oath.

"*Sacre bleu!* He is still alive."

At the sound of that voice, Juliet bit back a gasp.

"Ye said ye wanted him," Nasal Twang said. "Ye didn't say nofing about wanting him dead."

"*Nom de Dieu!* My instructions were to take care of him."

"Hey, now. I got nofing against giving a fellow a

good drubbing, like me and Ned give that baker in the village. But we don't do no killing, not for thirty quid we don't."

*The baker*! No! It was not true. Please heaven, let it not be true. Even as her brain denied the testimony of her ears, Juliet's insides conceded the facts by rolling like a wave at the seaside. Afraid she could not endure any more revelations without throwing up, she put her hand across her mouth.

"That's right," the man named Ned said, as if his partner had not been clear enough, "we don't do no killing unless there's somebody wanting to kill us first. Or arrest us. The excise men are always trying to catch us and take us to gaol, but—"

"*Cochon*! Imbeciles! Must I do everything myself?" When he received no answer, he said, "So be it. One of you give me your pistol, then stand aside and let us have done with this charade."

In the silence that followed, Juliet did not even breathe, fearing the sound would carry in the stillness. Then, to her horror, she heard the unmistakable sound of a pistol hammer being cocked.

"No!" she screamed, jumping up and stepping in front of the tree. "Please, Father. Do not kill him."

# Chapter Fourteen

*Tell the major that I will follow the kidnappers as closely as I dare.*

It was not to be wondered at that Juliet's message elicited an entire string of obscenities from Alex. "She is mad. Absolutely, certifiably insane! What was she thinking to take such a risk with her life?"

Since Ottway had been listening to similar animadversions on the young lady's sanity for the past twenty minutes, he offered no reply. Not that he was not concerned for her safety. He and Mr. Anthony Portman were every bit as frightened for Miss Moseby as was the major—and for Captain Lansdale as well.

Remembering the Frenchman's threat that very morning against the captain's life, it was not difficult to guess that this kidnapping was his doing. He'd hired two men to give a savage beating to the village baker, and it was possible he'd hired the same two malefactors to kidnap Captain Lansdale.

The question that gnawed at Ottway's brain, and that of the major's, too, he'd be bound, was *Would the kidnappers do murder?* And what of Miss Moseby? If they discovered her following them, what would those men do to her?

According to the groom who had run out to meet them the moment the curricle rolled onto the carriageway, the young lady had witnessed the two men dragging Captain Lansdale from the cottage and tossing him into a farm wagon. Then, after sending word up to the house about what had happened, she had ordered her horse saddled and had ridden out after the kidnappers.

It was a brave thing to do, and Ottway admired bravery wherever he encountered it, but he wished for her sake, and for the major's as well, that she had been a little less courageous. If she had only waited three minutes! That's how long the groom said she had been gone.

"Maybe less," he said. "Of course, the mare were fresh, not having been exercised today, on account of all the excitement this morning, so she took off at a gallop."

"Damnation!" Alex said. "Of all the stupid, idiotic things she could have done, none tops this."

He had never been so frightened in his life, or so angry with Juliet for putting herself in danger. When he found her, he would give himself the pleasure of wringing her neck. No! First he would kiss her, then he would throttle her.

For now, he vented his fear and his frustration by shouting at the groom. "Are you totally lacking in sense? How could you allow a young lady to go off alone like that? The stable is full of horses, could you not have saddled one of them and gone after her?"

"Alex," Tony said, pointing to the horse the groom had left standing near the doors to the stable. The horse was saddled and ready to go, as though the rider had been about to mount up when he spied the curricle.

Alex shook his head, hoping it might clear his brain. Forcing himself to speak calmly, he said, "I beg your pardon, Burt." Then, "Are you certain she went in the direction of the New Forest?"

"Yes, sir. Quite certain. And, Major," he said, reaching beneath his coat and pulling out a carriage pistol. "I took a few moments to load this."

"Good man," Alex said, reaching down and taking the pistol the groom held out to him. The weapon was cumbersome, and single-action, but it would be better than no weapon at all.

With no place to put the pistol, Alex passed it to Ottway, who sat in the small seat at the rear of the curricle. Unable to endure another moment's delay, Alex turned the curricle and snapped the ribbons, spurring the team into a canter, then into a gallop.

Under normal circumstances, a team of thorough-bred cattle would overtake a saddle horse in no time, but the pair were far from fresh and they were pulling a vehicle carrying three men. Even so, just before they reached the track where the alfresco party had turned off the other day, Alex thought he saw Juliet's mare disappear into the trees. "Was that her?"

"I believe it was, Major."

"And I believe," Tony said, "that you would be wise to bring this pair to a walk. It wouldn't do to overtake Juliet, and perhaps startle her or the mare. Or worse yet, let the kidnappers know we are behind them. Besides, you know the track ends at the smuggler's ditch."

Recognizing good advice when he heard it, Alex reined in the horses. The pair had not come to a complete stop when he jumped down and tossed the ribbons to Ottway. "My brother and I will go on ahead," he said. "As soon as you have the team secure, join us. But be careful. There is no knowing what we may find."

Alex did not wait for a reply. There was no need; he trusted Ottway with his life. The man was a battle-scarred veteran. His brother, now, there was a different matter entirely. Tony was a fearless sportsman, but a sportsman was not the same as a seasoned soldier. There was no way to know how he would react in the face of mortal danger, but for now Alex could not let that slow his own actions. He had to get to Juliet before the kidnappers realized she was there.

Using the thick trees for cover, he entered the forest as quickly and as quietly as possible, stopping only when he heard muffled voices up ahead.

"Over there," Tony whispered, pointing to a birch tree to their left. "Princess."

At first sight of the roan mare, Alex breathed a sigh of relief. His serenity was short-lived, however, for on looking more closely, he discovered that Juliet had left the animal and proceeded further down the path on foot.

He was definitely going to throttle her!

That thought had no more than flashed through Alex's brain when he heard her scream, "No!"

While he gulped deep breaths in hopes of keeping his heart inside his chest, he heard her once again. "Please, Father," she said. "Do not kill him."

Alex reached for the pistol the groom had given him, only to realize that he had not gotten it from Ottway. Damnation! With the element of surprise now his only weapon, Alex forced himself to move forward slowly until he saw Juliet up ahead. Her back was to him, but what made his blood run cold was that she faced Francois Du Monde, who held a carriage pistol in his hand.

On the ground at Du Monde's feet lay Geofrey Lansdale, bound and gagged, but still alive. Standing just a little way off were two very large men dressed like common laborers. One of them held a pocket pistol, a double-action weapon, though it was not aimed at anyone at the moment.

"What do we do?" Tony whispered.

Without a moment's hesitation, Alex said, "We get

them to shoot at us until their weapons are empty. Then we charge ahead."

"An excellent plan, brother. I have but one caveat. They have three bullets, while there are but two of us. What if that big fellow over there is a good shot, and he kills both of us? Du Monde will still have one bullet to spend on Lansdale, and there will be no one to stop him using it. We will have died in vain."

"Fool, I did not mean for the man to empty his weapon into us! I meant for us to make him shoot and miss."

"Ah, of course. What was I thinking? And your suggestion for making him miss?

After only a moment's thought, Alex smiled. "We play 'dropped pencil.' ''

Tony might never have been in battle, but he had played that prank often enough to need no instruction. While he stripped off his brown jacket and tossed it on the ground, his brother did the same with his green coat and waistcoat, leaving them both in similar white shirts and cravats. Alex's pantaloons were slightly darker than Tony's, but that could not be helped. Not that it would matter all that much in the slowly fading light.

"I do the dropping," Tony said. "After all, the original prank was my idea."

Not waiting for confirmation, he bent low to remain out of sight, then made his way eastward ten feet to a tree wide enough to hide behind. Once he was set, he nodded to Alex, who was behind a similar tree. At Alex's nod, Tony jumped from behind his tree, yelling, "Here I am!"

The large man, clearly startled by the sudden noise, lifted his weapon and fired, the bullet grazing the tree behind which Tony was again hidden.

The sound of the explosion was still echoing when Alex jumped from behind his tree. "You missed me!" he yelled.

"What!" The large man, thoroughly confused by the speed with which the intruder had gotten to a different tree, fired again. This time, the bullet went wide, missing Alex's tree by several feet.

"Missed again," Tony shouted, jumping out into the open, then back into hiding again.

"Ned," the man with the pistol said. "Did you see that? How . . . how fast he moved from tree to tree?"

"P . . . plumb uncanny, that," Ned said. "Almost like he weren't human."

Alex, pushing his advantage, stepped into the open. "Now what?" he taunted. "Do you mean to throw rocks at me? They can not hurt me, you know. One must be alive to feel pain."

He jumped back behind his tree, then signaled for his brother to remain hidden. Within no more than three seconds they heard the one called Ned swear, then turn and run toward the ditch, muttering something about the forest being haunted.

Taking his cue, Tony began to moan. The eerie sound made the remaining man shiver, but though he looked as if he wanted to run, something—pride perhaps—would not allow it.

"Ignore it," Du Monde yelled. "It is merely a trick."

When Alex began to moan as well, causing the ghostly sound to come from two places at once, the big fellow forsook all thoughts of pride and turned, running after his comrade. The sound of their mad scramble down the side of the ditch could be heard for a mile.

It was not to be wondered at that Francois Du Monde had not fallen for the trick, for he had seen the brothers together that morning, and knew there were two of them. "Come back!" he yelled at his hired henchmen. "It is all a trick, I tell you." When they did not return, but continued in their mad flight from the supposed ghosts, he aimed his pistol at Captain Lansdale's head. "I have not fired, so I have a shot left," he said, "and I will use it if you come one step closer. Either of you."

"Interesting," said a voice that came from a completely different direction, "for I be holding a pistol as well. If you discharge your weapon, I mean to do likewise. In which case, you will soon have a very large hole in your chest."

Ottway took a step forward, showing himself so there was no doubt that he possessed a weapon. While he held the carriage pistol pointed toward the Frenchman, Alex and Tony showed themselves in the clearing.

"Oh, Alex," Juliet said, her voice husky with fear, "were you harmed?"

"Hey!" Tony said. "What about me?"

"We are both whole," Alex said, then he held his arms out. "Now come to me, Juliet, if you please. Du Monde dare not shoot."

"*Mon Dieu!*" the Frenchman said. "Do you think I would harm my own daughter?"

To Alex's dismay, Juliet remained where she was. "Please," she said turning back to Du Monde, "has there not been enough violence? Can we not resolve this without anyone else getting hurt?"

While still aiming his pistol at the captain, Du Monde reached out with his free hand and cupped his daughter's chin. "Go. Please, *ma petite.*"

She shook her head. "I cannot. Not without Captain Lansdale."

"*Je regret,* but this has gone too far. I no longer have any opt—" He stopped short, for to his surprise, his daughter threw herself down upon the captain, covering his body with her own, her head shielding his. "Juliet, no!"

She looked up at him, and in her eyes was such pain that Du Monde felt as if the man aiming the gun at his heart had already fired.

"I beg of you," she said, "go. You must have a horse around here someplace. If not, take my mare, she is tied a short way down the track. Take her and ride away. Or follow those other two along the ditch. Go south and you will reach the sea where there are boats for hire."

"I cannot, *ma petite,* for the moment I move away from the captain, your friends will kill me. And I have no wish to die."

Surprising him again, Juliet stood and came to him, throwing her arms around his waist, shielding him as she had done the captain. "I will be your protection, Father. They will not shoot while I am before you."

She looked over her shoulder. "Alex, I am taking my father out of here. Will you let us go?"

One of the twins took a step forward, and Du Monde could only assume that it was the one his daughter had called Alex. "Du Monde," the fellow said, "there is no need for this. Let me come closer, where we can talk."

Du Monde allowed him to come forward, but stopped him before he was close enough to attempt to take the pistol. "I will not shoot your friend," he said. "You have my word as a gentleman."

"Oh, Father," Juliet said, hugging him for real and nuzzling her head beneath his chin. "I knew you could not."

Not taking his eyes off the man called Alex, Du Monde put his free arm around his daughter's shoulders, holding her tight for a few seconds; then, after kissing the top of her head, he pushed her hard, forcing her to release him. Not expecting such treatment, she tripped over the captain and fell at the other man's feet. "Take her," Du Monde said, "and look out for her, for I could not bear it if she came to any harm as a result of this day's work."

Alex pulled Juliet to her feet, then drew her into

the safety of his embrace. "Oh, my love," he said. "Never frighten me so again."

Without taking his eyes off his daughter, Du Monde reached inside his coat and pulled out a gold timepiece, then laid it on the ground beside his feet. "Your mother's portrait, *ma petite*. I want you to have it. Keep it to remember her by. And if you can, I beg you will remember me with at least a little kindness."

He began to back away, but he stopped when the man with the pistol stepped forward, his weapon raised and cocked, ready to shoot. "Not another step," the man said. "I thought sure I'd shot my last Frenchman when I left the army, but I'm more than willing to add one more Frenchie to the list."

"Ottway!"

"Yes, Major."

"Do not fire."

"But, sir. The man's a criminal. We know he had that baker beaten within an inch of his life, and he kidnapped Captain Lansdale. He's a fiend, and at the very least he deserves to be behind bars."

"I say again, Ottway. Do not fire. Let him be on his way."

"Happen Captain Lansdale will want to see the Frenchie pay for his crimes, Major."

"Then let the captain pursue him at some later date. For now, I wish you will put your weapon away. Would you have Miss Moseby witness her father's death?"

The Welshman looked at Juliet, whose face was wet with silent tears. "Reckon the young lady's had just about all she can handle for one day at that."

Slowly he eased the hammer of his pistol back into place. "Off with you then," he said to Du Monde, "before I change my mind."

Juliet watched as her father backed away, one slow step at a time, his pistol still at the ready in case Ottway should decide to shoot. When Du Monde was beside a thick clump of shrubs, he paused, blew Juliet a kiss, then stepped to the side and disappeared from sight.

Alex still held her in his arms, which was a good thing, because for the second time in her life, not to mention the second time that day, Juliet fainted.

# Chapter Fifteen

$\mathcal{J}$uliet welcomed the dawn with open arms, delighted to see the sky go from black to pearl gray to pinkish gray, and finally to clear pale blue. Yesterday had been the worst twenty-four hours of her life, beginning with the aborted departure from Portman Park, and ending with her being carried to her bed for the second time in a single day.

She was delighted to see that particular span of hours come to an end, and now she was just as happy to see the night follow it into oblivion. She had slept in twenty- and thirty-minute increments, waking each time with that lingering sense of alarm that comes with a bad dream. Only her terror had been no dream.

Small wonder that she wanted to be done with her attempts at peaceful repose.

"What you need is peaceful repose," Lady Feather had said last evening when Alex brought her home from the New Forest in his curricle. Tony had driven the farm wagon, with Captain Lansdale and Ottway as his passengers and Princess's sidesaddle tossed in the wagon bed. No one had said a word about the missing mare, so Juliet assumed her father had taken the little roan to make good his escape.

Alex's entrance into the vestibule at Portman Park, with her in his arms, had caused quite a stir. Lord Bevin, all four of the Quicks, and as many of the servants as could crowd into the small area hurried forward, all wanting to hear the story of the kidnapping. If Juliet thought they would be disappointed to see her, and not the captain, she was mistaken, for by this time everyone on the estate had heard how she had pursued the two men who took Geofrey Lansdale. They had heard, and they wanted to gawk, if only for the few seconds it took Alex to climb the stairs.

"Such shameless behavior in a female," Mrs. Quick said, not bothering to lower her voice. "Too coming by half. Of course, it would be foolish to expect ladylike behavior from a person of her background."

"Mama, please!" Miss Beatrice said. "I think she is a real heroine. Only consider how brave she was to pursue those—"

"I will thank you," said her mother, "to keep your opinions to yourself. I assure you, no one is the least interested in hearing them."

Thankfully, Juliet was spared any further comments, for by this time Alex had reached the top of the stairs. Lady Feather and Morag waited for her there, the look of relief on their faces easing away the worry lines that had probably grown steadily deeper over the past two hours.

"Bring her in here," Morag said. "I've kept the fire built up, and the bedcovers are turned down and waiting."

"Yes," Lady Feather said, "bring her on in, Major."

Not even attempting to hide the tears that coursed down her face, her ladyship reached out and caught Juliet's hand. "What a scare you gave us, my dear."

"I am sorry."

Juliet must have sounded rather pitiful, for Lady Feather turned away, as if needing to compose herself. After clearing her throat several times, she said, "No need to apologize, my dear, for you are home safe, and that is all that matters. Is it not, Morag?"

"It is that, your ladyship."

Lady Feather gave Juliet's hand a pat, then released
it and began shooing Alex out of the room. Over her
shoulder, she said, "Morag will get you tucked in bed,
my dear, and I will see to it that no one disturbs you.
After all you have endured this day, what you need
is peaceful repose. It is nature's panacea."

Panacea or not, Juliet had been unable to embrace
repose fully, and now, with the coming of dawn, she
was ready to abandon all further effort.

Morag must have heard her stirring, for the Scotswoman rushed out of the dressing room with such
speed that it was obvious she had never even tried to
sleep. Stopping beside the bed, she slid her arm beneath Juliet's shoulders to help her sit up. "Lean on
me, lass."

"Morag, please. I am not an invalid. Aside from
embarrassing myself by swooning—for which I blame
a diet consisting of nothing more than a triangle of
toast, a cup of chocolate, and a dosing of laudanum—
I am perfectly all right. I came to no harm yesterday.
At . . . at least, not physically."

She could not hide the sadness in her voice, and
hearing it, Morag advised her not to grieve. "And
above all, dinna let me see you hang your head as if
you've a reason to be ashamed. You are no more
responsible for what your father did than you are for
the cuckoo laying its egg in another bird's nest. What
he did or did not do was completely beyond your
control."

She fluffed the pillows so Juliet could sit more comfortably, then fetched the brush and began unbraiding
the thick plait. "You'll not believe me at the moment,
for you're young yet, but hearts do mend. Your mother's did, God rest her soul, and yours will too. Though
I never dreamed it would be the same scoundrel who
broke both hearts."

Morag could be infuriating at times, clucking about

like a mother hen, but in this instance she showed admirable restraint by allowing the subject of Francois Du Monde to drop. "Speaking of diets, I'll wager you could eat a wee bit of something."

"A *wee* bit? I could eat a horse, two sheep, and a goose with the down intact. And still have room left for a scone with jam."

They both laughed, and Morag gave it as her opinion that a person who could made a joke was already on the mend. "Which is probably more than can be said for Mrs. Quick this morning, for she'll be wearing a sour face I'll be bound."

"Oh? And why is that?"

The braid loose at last, Morag began to brush the long tresses, happy to relate what was—for her, at least—an enjoyable bit of gossip. "I dinna know the she-devil's exact words concerning your escapade, though I'm certain the remarks were spiteful. Still, anyone with ears in their head knows what Master Alex said later to Mr. Claude Quick."

Juliet gasped, remembering what one of his daughters had said several days ago, about Mr. Quick being excitable. "Never tell me that Alex challenged him to a duel."

"Nay, lass. Dinna be a goose. The gentleman is sixty-five if he's a day, and Master Alex—Major Portman, I should say—is too honorable a lad to take advantage of a man old enough to be his father."

Juliet breathed a sigh of relief. "He is honorable, is he not?"

"Aye," Morag said, drawing the syllable out, as if needing the time to consider a new and interesting thought.

Cursing herself for being so obvious, and hoping to remove that speculative look from Morag's eyes, Juliet returned to the subject of Mr. Claude Quick. "What did Alex say to him?"

"A few home truths. And high time, if you ask me."

While she finished brushing Juliet's hair, then tied it with a ribbon to keep it out of her face, Morag continued with her story. "He told Mr. Quick, did the major, that he was a poor excuse for a man, to let his wife come into a gentleman's home and utter spiteful things about her host's friends. Then he added that Mr. Quick was no kind of father, either, for he let his wife's bitterness against the world ruin their daughters' chances of making a decent match."

"Whew. There is plain speaking indeed."

Morag chuckled. "According to Mary, the maid as waits on the two young misses while they are here at the Park, Mr. Quick had a few home truths of his own to impart to his wife. And the upshot of it is that the Quicks are packing up to leave Portman Park today, instead of waiting for tomorrow, when they had originally planned to leave."

The talk of leaving reminded Juliet that she still needed to see to the hiring of a coach for the trip to Bath. When she said as much, and tried to get out of bed, Morag put her hand on Juliet's shoulder to detain her. "That's all been taken care of, lass. The major is seeing to the coach, and I've been given instructions not to let you fret about a thing."

As the morning wore on, Juliet discovered that being instructed not to fret, and actually not fretting, were two totally different matters. In truth, the only thing that broke in upon her constant worrying was the visits she received. Since Lady Feather and Morag ganged up on her and refused to allow her to leave her bedchamber, the visits were paid to Juliet in that intimate setting, with Morag sitting in the open doorway of the dressing room, playing combined chaperon and jailer.

The first visitors were Beatrice and Celeste Quick, who came to assure themselves that Juliet was well, and to tell her how much they had enjoyed making her acquaintance. She had enjoyed meeting them as well, and was genuine in her hope that they might keep in touch with one another.

"That could happen sooner than you think," Celeste said, giggling behind her hand. "Mr. Anthony Portman asked Bea if he might call upon her in the next week or so, and if he does, he could take any messages to and from Portman Park."

"Tony?"

Beatrice nodded. "He is a very nice gentleman, do you not agree?"

"Very nice," Juliet said. "Almost nice enough for you."

Beatrice blushed with pleasure at the compliment, while Celeste giggled again. "Bea has not told Mama yet, and I cannot wait to see the shock on her face when Tony comes driving up to our door."

*Poor Tony,* Juliet thought.

After exchanging hugs all around, the young ladies went belowstairs, and in a very short time Juliet heard the sound of coach wheels dislodging the crushed stone of the carriageway. The sound had only just faded into the distance when Juliet received her next caller, Captain Geofrey Lansdale.

That gentleman's visit, while no less welcome than that of the sisters, was far more distressing. After making her a gallant bow, he availed himself of the only chair, which stood beside the hearth, then began a long and impassioned expression of his gratitude to Juliet for having saved his life.

"Sir," she said, when he finally took a breath, "I assure you I did nothing but follow the wagon. It was Alex and Tony, with their foolish schoolboy prank, who saved the day. And Ottway, of course, for he alone possessed a weapon."

"Forgive me for contradicting you, ma'am, but even

though I am grateful to all three of those men for their part in my rescue, I cannot allow you to make light of your brave actions."

"Brave? Oh, no, Captain. If anything, I was petrified. Absolutely shaking with fear."

"I know that, Miss Moseby, for I felt your trembling when you lay your body down atop mine, to shield me from Worldly's bullet."

Clearly unable to remain still, the captain stood and strolled over to the window. Once there, he proceeded to turn the casement handle back and forth, nervously opening and shutting the window. Juliet barely noticed, for at the mention of Du Monde's alias, she remembered that it was to apologize to Captain Lansdale that she went outside yesterday.

"Sir," she began, her voice all but failing her, "I feel I must beg your forgiveness."

"Mine? Merciful heavens, ma'am, whatever for?"

She took a deep breath, hoping it would make her next words easier. Unfortunately, it did not. "Francois Du Monde—Frank Worldly, as you call him—is my father, and I—"

"Please," he said, leaving the window and coming to stand at the foot of her bed, "if you have any idea of taking that man's transgressions upon your shoulders, I beg you will not."

"But he had you beaten. And he came very close to murdering you."

"Which he did not, thanks to your intervention. In all truth, ma'am, had I been more responsible in my behavior while in London, had I not gambled beyond my ability to pay, none of this would have happened. The fault is entirely mine. If anyone should apologize, it is I, for bringing this calamity down upon your head."

Having said this, he shocked Juliet by coming around to the side of the bed and going down on one knee. Clearly wishing he were any place but here, he ran a finger inside his cravat as though it were choking him. "Miss Moseby," he said, "would you do me the honor of . . . that is to say, I wish to beg you to become my . . . "

He was obliged to swallow, and upon witnessing his Adam's apple bobbing up and down, up and down, Juliet began to suspect that some living creature had become trapped inside the captain's throat.

"My wife!" he finally managed to say, all but shouting the word in his push to get it past his lips.

If Juliet had not been so surprised, she might have laughed aloud, for if ever a man did *not* wish to propose marriage, that man was Geofrey Lansdale.

"Sir, I am persuaded that this quixotic gesture is prompted by some erroneous notion on your part that you owe me a debt of gratitude. Nothing could be further from the truth. And though I am sensible of the honor you do me by making me this offer, I really must decline it."

"But, ma'am, you were compromised, and all for my sake. As a gentleman, I cannot in good conscience allow your name to be—"

"She was not compromised, you jackass!" Alex said from the doorway, "now get up off your knee and quit making a damned cake of yourself."

It came as no surprise to Juliet that the captain took exception to both the intrusion and the name-calling. "Go away, Alex, for this is none of your concern," he said.

"Now that," Alex said, "is another one of your . . ." he looked at Juliet. "How did you put it, my love? Ah, yes. Another of your erroneous notions. Everything to do with Juliet is my concern, for I mean to marry her as soon as it can be arranged."

It was Hobson's choice as to who was more surprised by this announcement, the captain or Juliet.

When they both merely stared at Alex, he crossed the room, took his military friend by the arm, and more or less forced him to his feet.

"Here, now," the captain said, "take your hands off me."

Alex laughed, then gave his friend a playful punch on the jaw. "Go away, Geofrey, there's a good fellow. You made your offer, and Juliet refused. Now get out of here so that I can make mine. I mean to do it with a lot more finesse than you showed, and though you are in dire need of instruction, I do *not* mean to allow you to watch."

The look of abject relief on the captain's face was hardly flattering to Juliet, but she took it in good part, merely informing her "suitor" that she hoped to see him again before she left for Bath on the morrow.

The gentleman made her another bow, uttered something that sounded courteous, then made a hasty retreat from the room.

Without a word, Alex strolled to the door, closed it, then turned the key in the lock. Satisfied with that piece of impertinence, he walked over to the dressing room where Morag sat, her mouth open in astonishment at being privy to two proposals in the space of that many minutes. "Morag," Alex said, "you are my second favorite female in all the world, but I had better not find you listening at the keyhole." Having issued the order, he closed that door as well.

When he turned to look at Juliet, giving her a mischievous grin that was like the first day of summer— sunny and warm and full of promise—she felt her heart begin to dance, as if there were music playing inside her chest.

"And now," he said, "it is my turn to put my luck to the test."

# Chapter Sixteen

Juliet stared at Alex standing there beside the dressing-room door, overwhelmed by the joy it gave her just to be in the same room with him. The blue coat he wore made his eyes appear more gray than blue, and she found the change of color spellbinding. As well, the beautiful fit of his clothes accentuated the powerful body beneath, doing nothing to encourage Juliet to look away.

He was so handsome, and all she wanted to do was run to him and have him take her in his arms. She knew the feel of those strong arms, and just thinking about them holding her close gave her an unexpected ache.

Words of love formed themselves on her tongue, and it was all she could do to stop them from spilling out. She did stop them, however, for she knew that nothing good would come of this madness. She could not marry Alex. "It is impossible," she said.

"What is? That I could propose with finesse?"

"No. It is impossible for me to marry you."

The smile he gave her made a direct journey to her heart, causing it to beat dangerously fast in her chest. "Naturally," he said, "you cannot agree to marry me before I have the opportunity to propose."

"Oh, Alex, do not tease me. The reasons why I

cannot marry you are so obvious that I need not even mention them."

His smile disappeared. "The reasons are not obvious to me, so perhaps you had better mention them. Though, if the first one on your list is that you do not love me, and that you never could love me, then say so now and save yourself the trouble of reciting the entire list."

"I am a bastard," she said. "And worse than that, my father is . . ." She could not bring herself to continue. "You know what he is. And you know what people would say if you married Francois Du Monde's daughter."

"I care only for what you say, and so far I have not heard you say that you do not love me."

Juliet felt the tears burn her eyes. This was so much more difficult than she had thought it would be. "Lord Bevin will—"

"My grandfather may rant and rave, but he loves me as I love him, and he would never do anything to jeopardize that love. Besides, all you have to do is present him with a great-grandchild, and you will have him eating out of your hand. Give him two great-grandchildren, and before you can say 'Bob's your uncle' he will have you sitting for a portrait to hang in the gallery here at the Park."

As if suddenly remembering something, Alex reached inside his coat and removed a small object wrapped in plain white paper. "I went to the village first thing this morning and had this framed for you."

Even before he crossed the room to put the package in her hand, Juliet knew what it was. With trembling fingers, she folded back the paper. Inside was the miniature of her mother, the one her father had painted from memory, then kept encased in a gold timepiece. The thin layer of ivory had been refitted in a lovely silver filigree frame that was the perfect foil for her mother's blue eyes. The framing was beautifully done, but not as beautiful as the thoughtfulness behind the act.

"Oh, Alex. How can I ever thank you?"

"It is customary," he said, "for a lady to kiss a gentleman when he presents her with a gift."

A kiss. Juliet's heart ached to give him what he wanted—what she wanted as well—but still she hesitated. "Odd," she said, "but I have never heard of that custom."

"That is because it begins today."

Having said this, he sat down on the edge of her bed and took one of her hands in his. Turning it over, he brushed his strong, tan fingers back and forth slowly across her palm, allowing the pad of his thumb to caress the sensitive skin on the inside of her wrist.

For a moment, Juliet savored that gentle caress, and the warmth his slightest touch ignited in her. Then, before she realized what he meant to do, he bent toward her and brushed his lips against hers, arousing her senses and causing her to tingle all over, from the bottoms of her feet to the tips of her ears.

"When I heard you had ridden after those kidnappers," he said, mentioning that terrible episode at last, "my heart nearly failed me. I was practically paralyzed with fear, afraid I would lose you."

"You were?"

He brushed another kiss across her lips, and this time a warm sensation curled its way to the pit of her stomach, making her long for him to take her in his arms and make her forget everything but his kiss.

"You followed that wagon to the New Forest, and I followed you, and I spent the entire time promising myself that once I caught up with you I would kiss you first then throttle you afterward. And I may still throttle you."

It was odd, but when Juliet was at Miss Trillium's

Female Academy in Brighton, she had been taught that *throttle* was a synonym for *strangle* or *choke*. Alex must have learned an entirely different set of synonyms at Eton, for he put his hands not around her neck but on either side of her waist.

Before she realized his full intent, he had lifted her up off the mattress and settled her onto his lap. Following that, he gathered her in his arms and pulled her close against him. An instant later, his mouth came down on hers, making her forget all about synonyms and everything else she had ever learned at school.

What she wanted to know now, only Alex could teach her, and to her delight, he seemed more than willing to let the instruction begin. Again and again he kissed her, his lips making her forget all the sensible reasons why she must refuse to marry him, and allowing her to recall only one thing, that she loved him with all her heart, her soul, and her body.

When she finally reclaimed her lips long enough to draw a deep, restorative breath, Alex took that breath away again by whispering sweet words of love in her ear.

"I have never wanted anything in my entire life as much as I want you," he said. "And I have never loved anyone as much as I love you."

Alex felt her soft, sweet body tremble within his arms. He knew she loved him, she could not respond so if she did not.

"I have loved you for so long," he said, "that I can no longer remember a time when you did not fill my heart. All during the war years, it was your face I dreamed of at night. And afterward, when I knew I was coming home, the person I came home to was you. All my dreams of the future are filled with images of you. With the passion we can share, and the joy we can give to one another."

He touched his fingers to her lips, feeling their softness; wanting to feel them once again beneath his. "I need you, Juliet. Say you will marry me."

"I cannot," she said. "Surely you must see how ill-advised such a union would be."

"I see nothing of the sort, and starting right this minute, I mean to kiss you until you abandon this foolish notion that you must sacrifice your happiness as well as mine. Why should we care who some third party believes is a suitable partner and who is not?"

Making good on his threat, he drew her close and began to kiss her. Kiss after kiss until she moaned against his mouth. "Say it!" he said. "Say you will marry me."

When she did not obey his command, Alex caught her to him, molding her soft body to his. She was so warm, so sweet in his arms that he thought he would go insane with wanting her. "I love you," he said, then he brought his mouth down on hers, absorbing the sweetness of her, kissing her until he heard her moan with pleasure.

"I mean to wear away your resistance," he said, kissing her again.

When he finally let her breathe, she nestled her head against his shoulder. "I want to say yes," she whispered. "My heart aches to give you the answer you want."

He kissed her again, and this time, as he held her close, pressing her soft breasts against his chest, he felt her resistance melt away. "Marry me," he said again. "Otherwise, you doom me to a life of unhappiness, for I will never love anyone but you."

"Never is a long time."

"True, but that is exactly how long it would take me to forget you. To forget the way you laugh. The warmth of your smile. Your strength. Your indomitable spirit. The feel of you in my arms. The feel of this beautiful mouth responding to my kiss."

"Oh, Alex," she said, "you are the most wonderful

man in the world. And I cannot remember a time when I have not loved you."

"Is that your answer?"

"Half of it," she said.

"And the other half?"

She turned her face up and kissed his jaw, then the corners of his mouth, then finally she kissed him full on the lips. It was a soft kiss, yet so sweet it filled him with an intensity that was almost frightening.

He took her in his arms again. "I must hear the words."

"I will marry you, Alex."

"Again."

"I will marry you, Alex."

"Because . . . ?"

She giggled, and the sound was so enchanting that Alex had to remind himself that even a special license would require a few days to procure. And until that time, he would need to keep a tight rein on his desires.

"Because I love you, Alex Portman. I love you even more than I can say."

"Then do not waste words. Show me."

She slipped her arms around his neck, then kissed him so long and so sweetly that it nearly drove him wild. "Like that?" she asked.

"Yes," he said, his voice so husky he barely recognized it as his own, "exactly like that."

# About the Author

**Martha Kirkland** is a graduate of Georgia State University and a lifelong student of classical music. She shares a love of tennis with her husband, and a love of the ocean with her two daughters. As a soldier in the war against illiteracy, she volunteers two afternoons a week as a tutor in a local middle school.

# Allison Lane

"A FORMIDABLE TALENT...
MS. LANE NEVER FAILS TO
DELIVER THE GOODS."
—*ROMANTIC TIMES*

## Emily's Beau

0-451-20992-3

Emily Hughes has her sights set on one man:
Jacob Winters, Earl of Hawthorne. But her
hopes are dashed when she discovers that Jacob
is already betrothed. She will have to forget
Jacob and marry another, which is just what
she plans to do—until one moonlit kiss changes
everything.

### Also Available: